liberty
justice

BRETT
McKAY

Liberty Justice
Red Adept Publishing, LLC
104 Bugenfield Court
Garner, NC 27529
https://RedAdeptPublishing.com/

All poems, except for "Sometimes" and "Sunset," were written by Shanna Michelsen

Cover Art by Streetlight Graphics[1]

This is a work of fiction. Names, characters, places, and incidents either are the product of the author's imagination or are used fictitiously, and any resemblance to locales, events, business establishments, or actual persons—living or dead—is entirely coincidental.

---

1.   http://StreetlightGraphics.com

To all who suffer from addiction and those who are left in its wake

Brian,

Thank you for your interest in Liberty Justice. Hopefully we can work together and sell millions! I'm ~~eg~~ eager to hear what strategies you may have.

Enjoy

Brett M.

12-21-21

CHAPTER ONE

"Where's the damn tape? We outta tape?" Pete's voice shook the house, and in her room, Liberty Justice clutched her comforter tighter. She'd been asleep for only an hour when the screaming had begun. She listened as the argument escalated outside her bedroom.

"We only have the one roll. Is it all gone?" her mother, JJ, said.

"Yeah! There weren't but a couple a' inches left on it. Who used it last?"

Tingles ran up Liberty's spine, the hair on her arms erect, and fear dropped an anchor in her belly. Liberty had used the tape last, and she'd forgotten to put it on the list. That was his rule. If you ran out of something, it was your duty to write the item down so they would remember to get it the next time they went to the store.

She heard Pete stomp into the kitchen and the rumple of paper as he snatched something up.

"It ain't on the list!"

"Now, Pete. She just forgot, that's all."

"She supposed to write it down! How are we gonna wrap the rest of the damn presents?"

"Honey, it's Christmas. We'll find a—"

"Where is she?" He stormed out of the kitchen. "This is the last time! She needs a wuppin'!"

Liberty heard him rip his leather belt from the loops in his jeans. Her dog, Licorice, was lying on the floor beside her. Licorice popped her head up, ears perked, as Pete's steps pounded down the hall to her room. On her bed, Liberty pressed her back against the wall as far as she could. Licorice stood and released a bark.

"Liberty!" Pete hollered.

Boom! There was a massive thud as something hit the wall, and it was followed by several more muted thuds. Outside, her mother grunted as if she were trying to lift something heavy off of her.

Licorice barked again, ran to the door, then started to pace.

"Bitch!" Pete yelled.

"Don't you *touch* her!" JJ shouted.

More wails erupted, and limbs were slamming against the floor and walls. Violent slaps of skin against skin shocked Liberty, who realized she wasn't only crying but screaming.

Nails scratched at the door, and the knob moved slightly.

"You're not going in there!" Her mother stood her ground.

The fight outside her room continued for more grueling minutes. Howls, screams, curses, and thuds. Liberty pulled her covers up to her chin, clutching them tighter. Licorice barked twice but didn't budge from her sentinel spot. Liberty was thankful her dog was with her to protect her. *But what about Mom?* She wondered if this was the end. The violence and hatred that ignited the house and smothered the air like a blanket were as intense as a fire.

Pete was a large man—skinny, but he had some muscle to him. Liberty had felt the strength in his grip before, but it wasn't his most horrific feature. His eyes were. Once he started to drink, his eyes turned bloodshot, and his black pupils swam amidst the fractured white. There was madness in them. They drew you in, hypnotized you, and warned you that there was darkness inside. He wasn't just a man who lost his cool when his ego was hurt. He was the kind of man who wanted to see the world pay for what he was. A monster brimmed beneath the surface of his skin, waiting for any small crack to release it. Violence was the only thing that could fill the empty hole in his soul, and there was never enough of it.

An immense thud exploded and shook Liberty's body, and the door cracked in the center. She was certain they would not make it out of this one alive.

CHAPTER TWO

Seven Years Later

"Invisible"
I try so hard to fit in, but all they do is stare.
Is it the acne on my face, my worn-out clothes, or do they somehow
know of the secrets I hide?
If I could just be invisible, my life would be so much easier.
No more pain, no more lies, no more secrets...
-Poem from Liberty Justice's Diary

Liberty cracked her eyes open to a room shrouded in the last remnants of night. The sun struggled to rise and pierce the dark-blue shadows of her room. The clock read 6:27 a.m., three minutes before her alarm was set to blow. With a groan, she flopped her arm over and switched it off.

She pulled herself out of bed, stretched, yawned, then hobbled to the door on stiff legs. She heard cereal falling into a bowl from the other side of their mobile home. She closed her eyes and sighed because she knew it wasn't her mother getting breakfast. Liberty couldn't remember the last time JJ had woken up before noon.

Liberty stepped out and peeked into her mom's bedroom. Blackout shades were drawn. It was as dark as night, and JJ lay sleeping under a pile of crumpled blankets. Liberty rolled her eyes and continued to the kitchen.

Duke gulped down a giant spoonful of Cap'n Crunch with a slurp, and milk spilled down his chin. He wiped it with the back of his hand. Long, raggedy brown hair dangled over his bare shoulders, and tattoos covered most of his arms.

4

"Mornin', Sunshine," he said with a grimace as she walked into the kitchen.

"Morning, Thing," she grumbled, and he chuckled.

Thing was what she liked to call her mother's current boyfriend. Liberty's mom called him Jimmy, but she said it in baby talk. "Jim-myyy." It curdled Liberty's stomach.

"I have a name, you know. Jim Duke. You can call me Duke."

"I prefer Thing, thank you."

"You're a little spitfire, ain't cha?" A sly grin spread across his face. "That's what I love about your mom. She's a little spicy."

"Don't talk about my mom."

"Why?" He rested his elbow on the table and dangled the spoon above his cereal. "We've been seeing each other a long time now. Over a year. Hell, we're practically married. I could be—"

Liberty spun to face him and said, "There are three hundred and sixty-five days in a year. Of those three hundred and sixty-five days, you've spent twenty-two of them with my mom. That's not even a month."

"I *work*." He puffed his chest out. "I drive long-haul! I'm on the road!"

"Well, doesn't that make you boyfriend of the year!" Her eyebrows rose.

"Your mother loves me. An' I love her."

"Do you love the other women you spend time with while you're on the road?"

He glared back at her and scoffed. "You just got me all figured out, don't cha?" He lifted his hands, palms out, fingers splayed, and shook them wildly.

"It doesn't take a brain surgeon." She withdrew a bowl from the cupboard, a spoon from the drawer, and the box of Cap'n Crunch from the pantry. She shook the box. Only a handful of pieces bounced inside. She slammed it down on the counter. "You ate it all?"

"I'm a growing boy." He smiled. "There's eggs."

Glaring at him, she opened the fridge and grabbed the carton of eggs.

As she reached for a frying pan, he said, "Crack me a couple, too, will ya?"

Liberty snapped. She turned and threw an egg at him. He dodged, and it smashed against the wall. The yellow yolk and clear goo dripped amid shell fragments.

"You little shit." His face turned red, and his smile disappeared. Eyes enraged, he stood up and marched toward her with a pointed finger.

She flinched.

"I oughtta smack you!"

"Go ahead!" Liberty held the frying pan in both hands like a bat. "I smack back."

Silent, unmoving, they stared at each other. Wheels turned in his head as he contemplated his options. Then he seemed to think better of it and withdrew, waving her off.

"You are just like your momma. Stubborn." He sat back down with a laugh. "You know, I'm the closest thing you have to a daddy."

Liberty wanted to vomit.

"Least you could do is make me some eggs."

Liberty's face went hot. "It's the last thing I'd do," she mumbled.

Thing eyeballed her as she turned to make her eggs. "You're growin' up fine, you know? Pretty just like your mom."

Liberty shook, holding in the tears and rage.

"We're goin' to have to get along. 'Cause I'm not goin' nowhere."

"You're not leaving today?" Liberty asked.

"Oh, I'm leaving today, but I'll be back. I'll leave some money for your mom like I always do. I'm good that way. I take care of her."

That's your idea of taking care of her? Liberty thought. Out loud, she said, "Why don't you just not come back? It will be best for her in the long run. Really," she pleaded. "She needs to get better."

"Well, you're right about one thing. She's been pumpin' her veins full of that shit too much. I told her that."

"Yeah, but then you smoked crack with her last night!"

"That's just a little party! I don't do that shit every day. There's a difference. Adults need to do that from time to time. Life is tough out there, little girl. You'll see one day."

"It just keeps her sick. *You* keep her sick." Liberty trembled. "Please. This time, just go and stay gone. If not—"

"If not, what?" He pierced her with a sharp gaze.

Liberty stood strong, staring him down. "I'll call the cops on you the next time you come by."

"And tell them what?"

"That you're beating on my mom. They'll have to come. They'll search you and find the drugs."

Thing chuckled. "You'd never do that. Know why? 'Cause they'd take your momma away."

"I—" Shifting her attention to the floor, her words caught in her throat.

He pulled a cigarette out of his rumpled pack, lit it, then took a drag. He winked at her silence with a shrewd grin. "You know what happens when they take your mom away? They put you into foster care. You'll bounce from home to home with some of the worst fake mommies and daddies you'll ever see. And they'll beat on ya, just like they did me. Never love ya as much as they do their own kids 'cause they just do it to get money from the state, and the more messed up you are, the more money they get.

"You'll find out what you're really worth to people. I went through eleven homes before I finally ran away at fifteen and never looked back.

And your mom? Shit. You'll never see her again. Promise you that." He blew smoke into the stagnant air.

Tears spilled from Liberty's eyes. She avoided the urge to wipe them away, turning to crack eggs into the pan. She wouldn't give him the satisfaction of knowing he'd made her cry. That *Thing*.

Thing tapped his cigarette into an ashtray.

Scraping with intensity, Liberty stirred the eggs in the pan with a spatula.

"You goin' to school?"

His question seems so... normal. It made Liberty's skin crawl. Her answer was a flat, "Yes."

"What grade you at?"

"What grade are you *in*?" she corrected him. "I'm in eighth."

"Damn, you look like high school."

Gripping the spatula hard enough to turn her knuckles white, she mumbled, "Can we not talk? I thought you were leaving."

"All in good time." He put his cigarette down and slurped another spoonful of cereal.

Thing was no different than all the other guys Liberty's mom had brought home—skinny, wiry, ugly. They reeked of stale smoke and were always doped up on drugs. Cocky and ignorant, too, and with only one thing on their minds. Duke wasn't as bad as some. A couple of them had turned violent. Liberty thought of Pete and that horrific Christmas Eve seven years ago and shivered. Although Thing hadn't reached that violent stage, he had it in him. It was just a matter of time, and Liberty knew it.

Thing finished his cereal, stood up, and moved down the hall to crawl back into bed with her mom. Finally alone, Liberty ate her eggs in relative peace. The conversation and threat of violence played on repeat in her head, and she tried to push them to the back of her mind. Even after she finished eating and went to her room to get ready for school, she was shaken.

Determined to go about her day in serenity, Liberty stood in front of her open closet. There wasn't much to choose from, but one outfit stood out. She looked good in it, and it made her feel good too. It was the only outfit she owned that hadn't been purchased from Walmart or a discount store. Her mom's boss had allowed Liberty to work weekends bagging groceries. She'd spent months saving enough money to buy those designer clothes.

Once out of the shower, she wiped the condensation from the mirror and stared at her reflection with bleak expectations. She went to work on her hair with the blow-dryer and brush. To her surprise, everything fell into place. With a great outfit and a good hair day, she felt invincible.

When Liberty arrived at school, she walked the hall to her locker with poise. She didn't see Amanda, her best friend, but that was no surprise. Amanda was usually late to school.

Kate stood next to her locker, talking to three of her friends. She was tall, blond, and popular. Liberty and Kate ran in different crowds and rarely spoke to each other, but that day, Liberty felt stunning in her outfit and empty of her usual bitterness.

She smiled at Kate and said, "Hi."

"Hi," Kate grumbled, and glancing over her shoulder, she scanned Liberty from top to bottom. Her eyes went wide and rolled as she turned back to her friends. Murmuring under her breath, she said, "Three times this week with that outfit? Does she have anything else?"

Her friends chuckled. "I hope she at least washed it."

Their voices were quiet, as if that could keep Liberty from hearing them. The words hurt, just not immediately. She kept mental armor intact as she turned the combination back and forth on her locker, pretending not to hear. But the glow fell from her face, and her smile faded.

Locking her jaw and pursing her lips, Liberty turned to Kate. "I understand."

Kate raised a curled lip and squinted her eyes. "You understand what?"

"How you have to make fun of someone else to impress your fake friends. Then your bitches will follow you like sheep. I just find it funny, that's all."

For a moment, Kate's mouth went slack. Two of her friends glared, and the third shook her head, but Liberty didn't back down.

Kate finally chuckled and waved Liberty's comment away. "Nice try. Maybe if your mom sold heroin instead of using it, you could upgrade your home to a double-wide and afford better clothes."

Liberty's right fist flew in a blur and popped Kate's nose like a piston. In a flurry of waving arms, Kate flew off her feet then landed on her back.

Enraged, Kate's friend Sandy charged Liberty. Sandy reached out to tackle her, but Liberty's stance held strong. She twisted as Sandy collided with her, entangled her fingers in Sandy's black hair, then shot a knee into her stomach. Air escaped from Sandy's lungs in an audible *oof*, and she crumpled.

"Fucking bitch!" Alexis, one of Kate's other friends, screamed at Liberty and prepared to attack.

But from behind, someone grabbed her shoulders and threw her to the ground first.

Amanda stood over Alexis with gritted teeth and a hunger for a fight in her eyes. She shot a quick wink to Liberty then turned to the last girl standing. "Who's next?"

Kids quickly surrounded the scene to catch a glimpse of the fight, some of them chanting for more. Blood poured down the front of Kate's shirt as she pulled herself to her feet. She kept wiping her nose, but the flow didn't stop.

"Oh, I hope that's going to come out." Liberty pointed at her shirt. "Do you wash your clothes?"

Kate was speechless. All she could do was glare.

A teacher plowed through the crowd, demanding the kids head to class. Mrs. Squires grabbed Amanda's shirt, holding her back just as she lunged for Kate's other friend, who quickly backpedaled.

"Come on!" Spittle flew from Amanda's lips as she tried to pull away from Mrs. Squires.

Liberty turned to Kate as Mrs. Squires stepped between them.

"Break it up!" their teacher called out.

Liberty's gaze dropped to the floor as Mrs. Squires looked at her in shock.

Two more teachers quickly arrived, along with the vice principal. Within minutes, the crowd was gone. A teacher held a cloth to Kate's nose as she tipped her head back. Liberty and the rest of the girls were hauled off to the principal's office.

Mrs. Squires kept an arm around Amanda's shoulders as they walked side by side ahead of Liberty. Amanda craned her head back with a devious grin and raised her eyebrows.

Liberty nodded a thank you and smiled.

CHAPTER THREE

Vice Principal Hamlin leaned back in his chair, raised his eyebrows, and twitched his upper lip with a disappointed squeak. Mrs. Squires sat in silence next to Liberty like a gargoyle. Liberty kept her head down as she lifted her eyes to look at Hamlin.

"I'm surprised to see you sitting here, Liberty. You've never been in my office before."

She shifted her eyes back to the ground and nodded.

"I just looked up your grades. You're holding a 3.8 grade point average. Mrs. Squires says you're one of her best students."

"This is so unlike you." Mrs. Squires scrunched her eyes at Liberty and shook her head. "What happened?"

Liberty glanced at her with an embarrassed frown and shrugged.

"Why did you punch Kate in the nose? You could have broken it," Hamlin said.

"She just..." Liberty said. She couldn't find the right words. "She and her friends started it."

"How so?" Mrs. Squires asked.

"Kate was making fun of me, and her friends were laughing." Liberty scowled.

"What did she say?" Hamlin asked.

"Nothing." Liberty looked away again.

"I'm afraid that's not good enough." He leaned forward. "What exactly did she say to you, and what did you say back?"

"She made fun of my outfit."

"Your outfit?" Mrs. Squires asked, incredulous. "What is wrong with your outfit?"

"Exactly," Liberty agreed. "She said I wear it too much."

"So you punched her?" Hamlin asked.

"No." She didn't want to explain what had really caused her to hit Kate. The words were too painful, too embarrassing to repeat because deep down she knew they were true. But she was cornered, and she *had* to tell them. "She said that I was too poor to afford any other clothes. Then she made fun of my mom and where we live."

"Where do you live?" Hamlin asked.

Mrs. Squires stabbed him with a look that said, "What does it matter?"

"In a trailer park."

"So does half of Oklahoma." Hamlin shrugged.

Mrs. Squires placed a soft hand on her shoulder. "I get it, Liberty. I really do. Girls can be very mean, but you are above that. You can't let that get to you. You have too much to lose."

"We don't tolerate any violence here at Stillwater. It calls for immediate expulsion." Hamlin's chair squeaked as he rocked it back and forth and let those words sit in the air and sink.

Mrs. Squires's eyes widened, and tears welled up in Liberty's.

"I really should expel you. But..." He leaned forward again and looked at Mrs. Squires for help.

"Maybe a suspension?"

"Yes, a suspension," he agreed. "Five days should be sufficient, and when you return, you will have one month of detention. Is that understood?"

Liberty wiped tears from her eyes and nodded. They shared a few more words of life lessons with Liberty then dismissed her. Mrs. Squires followed her out.

Amanda, the short, feisty fighter, sat in a chair outside Hamlin's office, ready to be called in. She looked comfortable, like she'd been there before. She glanced up at Liberty. "Call me later, okay?"

Liberty nodded.

"You can go inside now," Mrs. Squires told Amanda, who stood up then stepped in.

The teacher turned back to Liberty. "You are one lucky girl." She smiled. "I can't believe he didn't expel you. We must have caught him on a good day."

"Yeah." Liberty half smiled.

"Take this time to study. I'll send you home with next week's work."

"Okay. Thank you."

"And keep working on your poetry. You really have a gift. I still think you should enter the state writing contest."

"I will."

The teacher turned to walk back into Hamlin's office when Liberty stopped her.

"Mrs. Squires." When she looked back, Liberty said, "Thank you. I owe you."

"You do the work I told you about, and that's my payment."

LIBERTY SAT WITH HER back against a tree and thumbed through her notebook. She couldn't return to class, so she posted herself in the front lawn area next to the entrance and waited for Amanda to bounce through the doors. She was sure to get the same punishment.

The grass was cool, and a breeze blew softly against her. She glanced over several poems she'd written. Most of them contained scribbled or crossed-out words. Some had been jotted down in a rush, and others had been constructed with precision. She found an empty spot and let her pen do the work. The minute it touched the paper, the words and passion emerged and spilled onto the page. That was how it always was for her.

Sometimes.

I don't belong.

I'm not like them.

I'm empty. I'm hurt. I'm special. I'm nothing. I'm pretty. I'm pissed. I'm ugly.

Am I like them? Do I want to be like them? Sometimes.

"Liberty." Amanda trotted down the steps of the entrance toward her.

Liberty wiped away an escaping tear and looked up to greet her friend with a smile. The mischievous grin on Amanda's face made it hard not to lighten up.

"You get suspended too?" Amanda asked.

Liberty nodded.

"Welcome to my world."

"What do we do now?"

Amanda's smile took up half of her face, and her eyebrows moved up and down. "Free day, baby."

Liberty thought of her mom and Jim Duke at home. She pictured them still in bed, smoking crack together. "We can't go to my place."

"Both my foster parents are at work. The only one at home is their son, Roger, and he just plays video games all day. We can hang out there," Amanda offered, and Liberty agreed. "But first, let's get some food. I'm hungry. Got any lunch money?"

Liberty thought of the money she'd grabbed from her mom's dresser before leaving for school. She was going to use it to buy groceries, but she figured she could use a bit to eat out. "Yeah, I got some."

The two left the school grounds and walked in the direction of Amanda's home. They stopped at the Waffle House on the way. The light for the *W* was out on the sign, and they laughed about how it looked more like how the food tasted. Awful House.

"I still can't believe you punched out Kate." Amanda shook her head as she dug into her hash browns.

Liberty chuckled. "I have to admit—it did feel pretty good."

"What a piece of shit to say that about your mom."

"I know." Liberty's voice came out in a low tone. The truth behind Kate's words had caused real pain. In her mind, the trouble at home had stayed in a bubble that no one else knew about. She could deal with bullies at school if her issues stayed private, but to hear Kate speak of it meant the secret was out.

She took a bite of her scrambled eggs and ham and washed it down with chocolate milk. "How's life at your foster home?"

Amanda shrugged. "Okay, I guess. They have a lot of strict rules that are a pain in the ass. They don't allow any swearing in the house, and you know my mouth. I get in trouble a lot."

"I get that. I lived with my aunt for a while, and she was really strict about language too."

"I can't even say 'shit' in the house." Amanda guffawed. "They can say 'shit' on TV! I think anything allowed on TV, you should be able to say. And they give us chores to do and curfews, but they're actually pretty nice. A lot better than the last home I stayed in. Those guys were real assholes."

"My mom's dating an asshole. Again," Liberty grumbled.

"She still with that Jim Duke guy?"

Liberty nodded. "He's no good to her. He makes everything worse. There's just something about him I don't trust. Like he's plotting something, you know?"

"Parents do crazy shit." Amanda shook her head. "Look at my parents. Who abandons their kid when they're five years old? I'm startin' to think there isn't such a thing as a good parent."

Liberty looked out the window then, after a moment, said, "Mine use to be."

CHAPTER FOUR

Detective Clay Baxter sat across from Daryl Holmes in the small interrogation room. Daryl was a prime suspect in a robbery and homicide investigation. They'd spent over five hours questioning him that day, and Clay saw the exhaustion in Daryl's features. His barriers were coming down. He'd been brought in once before for an interview as a possible suspect, but since that time, new evidence had turned up and pointed in Daryl's direction. Clay was on the cusp of Daryl's confession. Twenty-five years of experience, along with his gut instincts, told Clay that Daryl was about to break.

"Listen," Clay said softly, "I really want to help you out here."

Daryl, looking off to his left, gave Clay a side-glance and shifted his eyes with a grunt.

"We've spent hours going over the events of April ninth. We need to finish this. Tell me what happened."

"I've told you a million times. What else do you want me to say?" Daryl crossed his arms.

"The truth. Let's try that for once."

"I *have* told you the truth!"

"No. You've told me three different stories," Clay said.

Daryl shook his head with a smug chuckle and leaned back.

"In the first story, you weren't even there. You said you were at home."

"I told you the truth when you brought me in this mornin'."

"Yes, but only after we found DNA evidence proving you were there and your friend ratted you out."

"And that ain't enough?" Daryl asked.

"It's just not the whole truth. This morning, you said it was Barnes who ordered the manager to empty the till, and you stood in the back. Then you said it was also Barnes who filled the bag with cash while you kept the customers covered with your shotgun. I asked what type of gun Barnes held, and you said a forty-five pistol. Am I correct?"

"No." Daryl scowled. "Barnes had the shotgun."

"That's what you told us in your second story when you spoke to Detective Calloway. Do you see what I'm getting at?"

Daryl rolled his eyes.

"*You* had the shotgun in your first story. Then you said it was Barnes. Which is it?"

"Barnes had the shotgun. The whole time. Must a' made a mistake when I told you the first time, but no, Barnes carried the shotgun. Not me. Sorry 'bout that."

"So, while Barnes shoveled cash into the bag, the manager reached for a gun, and that's when you say Barnes shot him?"

"Dat's right." Daryl nodded.

"It doesn't add up. It takes two hands to put cash in a bag, which would mean Barnes would have to either set the shotgun down or hold it under his arm. Then, while holding the bag in one hand, turn and shoot the man one-handed with the shotgun?"

"Well... sorta. I think he put the bag down first."

"Daryl." Clay leaned forward. "Let's cut through the bullshit. Keith Jones was shot and killed by a shotgun. That's why you changed your story. If you're telling the truth, it never changes. But when you make shit up, stories shift and change."

"It wasn't me!"

"The shotgun pellets hit his chest from about fifteen feet away. Not close-up. Not where Barnes was." Clay set a number of pictures on the table and pointed to each one as he spoke. "This is the manager, Keith Jones."

Daryl glanced at it then looked away.

"This is his wife. This is his six-year-old daughter, Sienna. And this is the whole family together."

Daryl continued to avert his eyes.

"Look at them," Clay demanded.

Daryl shook his head.

"*Look.*"

Daryl twisted his head and peered down at the images. He held his gaze on them for a few seconds, lifted them to Clay in defiance, then turned away.

"Brianne misses her husband. Sienna has a daddy who will *never* come home again." Clay saw tears well up in Daryl's eyes, and Clay knew he was getting to him. "You have a daughter, don't you?"

Daryl nodded. "She's five."

"You'll be gone for a long time, but your daughter still has her daddy. Sienna never will."

"I didn't mean for him to get killed." Daryl's shoulders sank, and he let out a breath of pent-up tension.

"I know you didn't," Clay said empathetically.

"He pulled a gun. He was going to shoot Barnes. I told him not to reach for a gun. We warned him to not do anything stupid. I yelled it at least three times! Fucking fool didn't listen!" Daryl's voice cracked.

Clay sat back and kept silent as Daryl wiped tears from his eyes. Clay turned to the camera in the corner, where he knew his lieutenant and partner were watching. He gave them a nod.

CHAPTER FIVE

Liberty spent the rest of the day at Amanda's house, mostly gossiping and listening to music. She left around three o'clock, walked a few blocks, then headed for the nearest supermarket, Happy Service. Her mother worked there part-time. There was no food in the house, and they needed dinner. She knew her mother hadn't gone to the store. It had become a consistent duty of Liberty's.

It took her only fifteen minutes to grab enough food to stretch out for the rest of the week. Hamburger Helper, boxes of macaroni and cheese, hot dogs and buns, ravioli, one pound of ground beef, orange juice, milk, eggs, bread, and a box of cereal—Cocoa Puffs, her favorite. She also threw in a box of cookies and a package of Lemonheads.

"Hi, Lib. How're ya doin'?" Bobbi smiled as she rang Liberty's items through the checkout stand. She was a coworker and friend of Liberty's mom.

"Good, Bobbi. How're you?"

"Good. Real good. How's yer mom? She feelin' better?"

The question caught Liberty off guard. She wasn't sure how to answer. *Maybe she was supposed to work but called in sick?*

"She's pretty sick. I think it'll pass soon," Liberty lied.

"She got the bug? It's been goin' around, I tell ya. Hank and Larry both got it real bad. She probably got it from them."

"Yeah, probably." Liberty nodded.

She watched the increasing number on the register anxiously. She held thirty-two dollars in her pocket and hoped it would be enough. The number was already in the midtwenties, and quite a few items remained to be rung up.

"I didn't mean to grab those"—Liberty gestured to the cookies and Lemonheads— "Sorry. I don't know what I was thinking." She offered Bobbi a weak smile.

Bobbi picked up the items. "You don't want these?"

"No, sorry."

"You sure? That's the good stuff." She grinned. "Tell ya what. I'll cover 'em." She winked and lifted the items to put them in her bag.

Liberty stopped her. "It's just that... I'm on a diet. I gotta watch my figure. I better not."

Bobbi nodded. "Okay. I gotcha. I'm supposed to be starting Weight Watchers on Monday myself. But then again, I been goin' to start that for nine weeks now." She broke out in a loud laugh.

Liberty gave her a courtesy smile and chuckled.

She set them aside and totaled the items. "Thirty-one sixty."

Liberty walked three blocks to her house, holding the plastic shopping bags. The weight of the straps dug into the palms of her hands, and her arms went numb.

She didn't see Duke's truck out front, which was a good sign. She entered the dark house of cheap paneled walls and shag carpet, and it was cloudy. The cigarette smoke sucked all the oxygen out of the room.

JJ sat hunched over on the couch, watching TV. Her long dirty-blond hair draped over her shoulders, and she flicked a cigarette in the fingers of her right hand. Despite her ratty tank top and baggy gym pants, she was still a pretty woman. Large blue eyes, high cheek bones, and a slim figure. Although, she could use more meat on her bones. The problem was, she could be much prettier. There'd been moments when she had been clean and healthy and could stop a clock. Instead, her arms were purple and bruised from drug use, her skin was covered in red sores and acne, and her unwashed hair and body odor reeked with that damn cigarette smoke, which made it impossible to breathe. JJ could be so much more than the mother Liberty saw on the couch.

"Hi, sweetie," her mother's cracked voice spoke.

"Is he here?"

"Jimmy? No, no. You made sure of that."

Liberty sensed the disdain in her voice. She crossed into the kitchen and commenced putting the groceries away. "What does *that* mean?"

"He told me about your little conversation this morning. You really pissed him off."

Liberty shook her head. "I pissed him off? Right."

"What did you say to him?"

"He ate all the cereal that was left."

"*Liberty.* Really? Cereal? Come on. He's a guest in this house, and he can eat our cereal, for hell's sake. Don't tell me you riled him up over that."

"I riled him up?" Liberty charged into the living room. "You two have partied this whole week! Eating food, leaving garbage, smokin' your crack, and having a good ol' time. Leaving me to clean up after both of you!"

JJ looked up at her from the couch with softened eyes, and a smile crept at the corners of her mouth. "I'm sorry, sweetie. You do take good care of me."

Liberty stayed silent. JJ was mocking her. Liberty wanted to bolt.

"It's true." JJ stamped out her cigarette in the ashtray on the coffee table. "We left a mess." She stood up, walked over to Liberty, and wrapped her arms around her.

Clenching her fists at the mockery in JJ's tone, Liberty did not return the hug.

"It's too bad," she whispered in Liberty's ear, "that you have a roof over your head, clothes to wear, and food to eat."

Liberty pushed her away. "Food? The food that I had to go get because there's nothing here? Duke ate us out of everything!"

"Food that you got with my money! Don't think I didn't notice the cash gone from my dresser." JJ's eyes accused.

"Well, how did you expect us to eat tonight? You weren't going to get it."

"I was going to. How do you know I didn't have other plans? You left me here without any money. How am I supposed to go to the store?"

"I don't know. You're the mom." She turned to walk away.

JJ pulled her back by her arm. "Don't talk to me that way, young lady. I *am* still your mother."

"Then try acting like one!" Tears came to Liberty's eyes, and she yanked her arm from her mother's grasp and walked out of the room. "And he was leaving anyway. Like he always does. He certainly didn't leave because I hurt his little feelers."

"Jimmy is good to us. I don't understand why you don't like him."

"Ugh." Liberty sighed. "Did he leave us any money? He said he was going to."

"He left me some."

"Some? So you did have money, but you didn't go to the store?"

"I planned to later. I'm still not feeling well." The tone of her voice softened to a whimper. "Still got this damn cold, and my head won't stop pounding."

Liberty resumed emptying the shopping bags and putting the groceries away.

"What did you get from the store? Anything good?" JJ asked.

"Just some stuff. We should get by for a few days with it. What are we having for dinner?"

JJ walked to her daughter from behind and stroked her hair. "Liberty."

She didn't answer.

"I am *sorry*. I didn't mean to yell at you. You know I love you."

Liberty turned, and JJ hugged her. "I love you, too, Mom."

"Love you more."

"Love you mostest."

"Still love you more."

The "love you more," and "love you mostest" back and forth had started when Liberty was a little girl. When things got ugly and out of hand, her mom stopped, wrapped her in her arms, and they argued about who loved who more. It almost always snapped them out of a bad mood.

Her mom pulled back and said, "Let's order pizza tonight! I don't want to cook, and I don't want you to have to either."

"Okay." Liberty smiled. "Sounds good."

JJ's eyes shifted away as she said, "You got this okay in here, Lib? I've got to use the bathroom. I'll be a little bit."

Liberty knew what that meant. Her mom had to go shoot heroin. She always did it in the bathroom like it was a dirty secret.

"Mom, do you really have to? Tonight?"

JJ scratched her head, and her eyes darted around the room—everywhere but in Liberty's direction. "Honey, you know I do. I'm sick. It's a sickness. I need to get well. Before I get withdrawals and get ill. You don't want to see that."

Liberty had before. It would be nothing new, but she agreed with her mom. She didn't want to witness her mom's withdrawals again.

"Do you want me to order the pizza?"

"Yeah. Go ahead. Money's in my purse," she said as she walked down the hall.

CHAPTER SIX

Liberty sat disgusted as she watched her mother on the couch, eyes rolling into the back of her skull, her body wavering back and forth like a weed in the wind.

"Geez, Mom. You look like a medium in a séance summoning the dead."

JJ's eyes slowly focused on Liberty, and a lazy smile crept up her face. "My Liberty. Always crackin' a joke." Her words were slurred, but she managed a chuckle. "Kind of a biting humor you got though."

"Look at my inspiration." Liberty glowered as she switched TV channels from her chair.

"Is the pizza here yet?" JJ asked.

"No, and it's been almost forty minutes. I'm about ready to call them."

"Call 'em! Want me to? I'll call the bastards."

"As entertaining as that would be, no, thank you." She held up her palm, signaling her mother to stop. "I got it."

Another ten minutes went by, and Liberty picked up her phone to call when the doorbell rang.

"Wha—" JJ popped up out of her stupor.

"Finally." Liberty set her phone down and jumped up. "Pizza's here."

JJ slumped back into the chair.

Liberty opened the door. The man who stood before her wore a leather jacket and jeans, and his long hair draped over his eyes. He was bent forward as if he'd run five miles and was catching his breath. He squinted at Liberty, and his upper lip rose in question.

Liberty was perplexed. Something didn't seem right. He wasn't carrying a pizza.

"Where's the pizza?" Liberty gestured with her palms up.

"Pizza?" He sounded confused. He pushed the hair out of his face, and that was when Liberty saw the purple swollen eye and cut on his forehead. Blood dripped from the wound. The right side of his lip was fatter than the other and wet with crimson, and sweat glistened on his face. He leaned forward, stretched his neck, and looked both ways as if crossing a street. Then he pushed his way in. "Where's your mom, little girl?"

"Hey!" Liberty jumped in front of him, forcing him to stop. "Are you the pizza guy?"

Ignoring her, the man craned his head and saw JJ on the couch. "JJ!" He pushed past Liberty, still looking side to side as if there might be more people in the house. "Where's your boyfriend?"

Cigarette dangling between her fingers, JJ looked up at him with a sleepy grin. "*Billy Ray?* What're you doin' here?" JJ's slow drawl came out.

"You know damn well what I'm doin' here." The man called Billy Ray scanned the room.

"What're you doin' in my house? You're not supposed to be here." JJ's brow wrinkled.

"Mom? What is he talkin' about? W-Who is this guy?" Liberty's voice cracked. Her head began to spin.

"You and that boyfriend of yours *stole* from me." He pointed an accusing finger.

"*Mom?*" Liberty's voice shook. The world in front of her blurred. *What is going on?*

"That big ass boyfriend a' yers beat the shit outta me and left me like this on the side a' the road!" Billy Ray towered over JJ, his arms out like a cowboy ready to draw.

"What are you talking about?" JJ sat up straight and cocked her head to the side. "We paid you." Her words came out slow, and she strained to annunciate the words.

"That's impossible. She's been here the whole time," Liberty added.

He wiped the blood from his lip with the back of his hand, turned, and glared at Liberty.

"Her boyfriend left hours ago. I've been here with her the whole time." She pointed at her mom.

"You don't know your motha' like I do." He pulled a sly grin and licked more blood from his lips. "Her and her boyfriend came by earlier to buy. Not to my dealers on the street, mind you. No, they came to my place of business. On the day I'm collectin'." He turned back to JJ. "I saw your boyfriend eyeing my bag of cash. You two were scoping me out, plannin' to roll me. Ain't that right, JJ?"

Liberty saw a pistol sticking out of the back of his pants. Her heart leaped into her throat. She quietly backed into the kitchen. Out of sight, Liberty picked up the landline phone on the wall. There was no sound. It was dead. *Did he cut the phone line before knocking on our door?* Either that or the service was turned off for lack of payment. She had a sudden urge to pee.

Where's my iPhone? Her mother had given her the used smartphone a few months back. Liberty didn't bother to find out if it was stolen or how her mom had come about it, but the gift was so uncommon that Liberty never let it out of her sight. She turned with panicked eyes and searched the kitchen. She didn't find it in there.

Liberty ran back into the living room in time to see Billy Ray grab JJ by the tank top and pull her to her feet.

He pushed his face into JJ's. "What did you do with my money, bitch?"

JJ squinted and made a sour look as if his breath reeked. Her eyes rolled like logs on water. She was still in her euphoric state but fighting to sober out of it. He slapped her quick and hard across the cheek.

The sound of the skin-on-skin slap stilled Liberty's heart. Christmas Eve with Pete flashed in her mind. Suddenly, she knew where her phone was—sitting on the arm of the couch. On the other side of *him*.

He slapped JJ again. "You think you can get away with it?"

"What money? I didn't do anything!"

Billy Ray threw her across the room. Her body twisted, and her elbow banged against the TV, knocking it over.

Liberty ran back into the kitchen to find a weapon. She grabbed what she was looking for, sprinted to the front room, then halted.

Billy Ray stood over JJ. Rage filled his eyes, and his chest pumped in and out. He screamed and kicked her in the stomach. She coughed out milky bile then gasped.

An iron skillet clutched in her hands, Liberty ran at Billy Ray as he reached for the gun in his pants. Liberty swung. There was a loud *clang* as the pan hit his knuckles and the gun. The pistol fell to the ground and rolled out of sight. Billy Ray yelped and clasped his hand. He snapped around to Liberty, who shook but held her stance, ready to swing again.

"It's time you leave," Liberty said.

He faked a lunge, causing her to flinch. Then he sprang on Liberty, grabbed her before she could swing, and threw her. She flew, landed on the couch, rolled off, then slammed into the coffee table. Trinkets, cups, and magazines toppled, and the glass inside the table cracked.

Billy Ray turned back to JJ, who was on all fours catching her breath. He tangled his hands in her stringy hair and kneed the side of her head. The other side of her head banged against a nearby recliner. He threw punches into her body.

"No! Stop it!" Those were all the words Liberty could manage.

She picked herself up, ran at him, then aimed the pan at his back. He turned, caught Liberty by her head, then pushed her down. As Liberty fell backward, JJ cried out and clamped her jaw around his ankle. She bit hard enough to break the skin, and blood ran through her teeth.

"Bitch!" he yelled and kicked three times before shaking JJ off.

He looked around the living room. When he couldn't find his gun, he withdrew a shiny, curved knife. Billy Ray raised it, and JJ cowered with hands outstretched and horror in her eyes.

Bam! Billy's head shook, and he touched the back of his scalp. His hand came away red. He turned with a snarl. Liberty, angry and intense, stood ready to swing the pan again.

He lunged for her with his knife. Backpedaling, Liberty tripped and fell. But Billy Ray's left leg was tangled with JJ's, and as he pulled free, he, too, tumbled. At the same time, Liberty threw the skillet. The pan clanged against his right shin, and he yelped. Arms flailing, Billy Ray's footing failed. Hands out in front of him, he toppled over Liberty, then she heard him smash into the fractured coffee table.

There was a moment of deafening silence. The fray was at a halt, but it took Liberty and JJ a moment to realize the attack had ceased. Billy Ray wasn't hovering over them, swinging his knife, and yelling.

Liberty sat up. JJ's eyes were open wide, looking past her. Liberty followed her gaze.

Billy Ray was lying half off the coffee table, one arm dangling. His body was facedown, but his head looked strange. It was as if he'd lain down on his stomach and rested his chin on the end of the coffee table so his head was up to watch TV. His legs convulsed, and so did his arms, and there was a horrible gurgling sound like a clogged drain. Something trickled down the side of the table. Dark crimson spread on the carpet.

The knife! Where is it? Liberty looked frantically. *I'd better grab it before he comes to.* She didn't see it or the gun anywhere. She moved closer. The sporadic twitching of his body slowed down. Then she found the knife.

The blade was lodged in his throat to the hilt. It had entered from the underside of his chin, and the handle pressed against the table, holding his head steady. Billy Ray choked on the blood pouring through his open wound. His frightened eyes, almost childlike, seemed to turn to Liberty for help. Then his body finally stopped jerking, and his eyes froze.

CHAPTER SEVEN

"**M**om!" Liberty ran to JJ's side. "Mom! Are you okay?"

JJ had a dazed look as Liberty helped her to her feet. JJ put a palm to her head, sighed, then nodded. "I'm good."

"We gotta get outta here. Fast!"

Dogs barked from several of the neighbors' homes, and porch lights turned on next door. Their commotion had been loud enough to cause concern. Cops would be called. The police would come. They'd be taken into custody. They'd find JJ high on heroin and her stash if she still had it. *And a dead drug dealer on our floor.* Child protective services would get involved. Her mom would serve time. Being a minor, Liberty would make out fine. Maybe. She wasn't sure. She'd killed someone. Self-defense, yes, but she didn't know if they would see it that way.

Whether Liberty served time or not, one thing was for sure—she would never see her mother again. She would be thrown into foster care. Bounced from home to home like Amanda. Like *Jimmy* Duke had. Amanda had spent many nights telling Liberty nightmare tales of the people she'd lived with. She'd seen the fear and trauma in Amanda's eyes as she told them.

Liberty's aunt, Serene, popped into her head. She might be able to go stay with her, but that thought made her stomach curdle. Liberty had no time to think or contemplate. It was now or never. Despite her body shaking and the whirlwind in her head, her survival mode kicked in.

"Come on, Mom. Grab what you can. Take only what you *really* need."

Still in a stupor and quivering, JJ nodded.

Liberty threw several food items together in shopping bags, including some necessary utensils and a can opener. She pulled out the only suitcase they owned, beat up and shabby, and threw as many clothes in as she thought they would need. She gathered clothes for her mother, too, while JJ wandered the house like a zombie.

"Mom? Are you getting stuff together?"

"Yeah. I'm workin' on it."

"We have to hurry!"

JJ disappeared into the bathroom. Items clanked as she put several things into a bag. It never failed. Her mom's priorities were in there. Her syringe, lighter, spoon, rubber strap, and all her stash.

Liberty searched JJ's hiding spots and grabbed as much cash as she could find.

"Cops are going to come," Liberty said while her mom stood in the bedroom doorway. Liberty zipped up the suitcase.

JJ's face twisted, and she started sobbing. Her shaking hand went to her mouth. "We killed someone. There's a dead man in our house."

"Mom." Liberty trotted over to her, pulling the suitcase behind. "He was going to kill us, remember? It was self-defense. But when the cops show up, they're going to arrest you, and..." Liberty's voice trailed off as her lips trembled and tears approached. She took a deep breath and held them back. "They'll take you away. That's why we have to go. Okay?"

Eyes closed, JJ nodded.

As Liberty threw everything into the back of their 2008 Dodge Caravan, she heard sirens in the distance.

At the last minute, Liberty grabbed their camping gear—a tent, cookware, and two sleeping bags. JJ wavered on the porch steps with a dazed look in her eyes. Her body was still coming down.

There was sudden horror in JJ's eyes. "I can't drive."

"I know, Mom. You get into the passenger side." Liberty opened the door and helped her in as the sirens got closer.

Liberty ran around the van then hopped into the driver's side. She adjusted the seat so her legs could touch the pedals, started the engine, put it in reverse, then hit the gas. The van jetted back, and Liberty slammed on the brake pedal, jolting them. She'd tried driving only twice. Up and down the street wasn't enough experience for what she was about to attempt.

She moved the gear to drive, gently put her toe on the gas, then slowly drove down the street. The first turn was a little tricky and bumpy, but she made it. She took a deep breath and continued. It was so dark, and it was hard to see. Then she realized her headlights weren't on.

"Lights! Where are the lights?" Panic clouded her thoughts.

"Turn the knob on the left." JJ pointed.

She found it, and her trembling fingers turned the knob. Lights illuminated the road ahead.

As she approached the exit to the trailer park, she saw the red flashing lights in the distance. She turned and headed in the opposite direction.

Are you okay? she asked herself and began a private conversation in her head.

No. I'm not okay.

Is this the best decision? The cops are going to find you. They always do.

I know. I know!

She grunted, sighed, then glanced at her mom. JJ's head was tilted back against the seat, mouth gaping wide. She was out. The immediate danger was not enough to sober her.

Then why are you running?

Time to think. I just need time to think!

Think about what?

How to get out of this mess.

The other voice was silent for a moment. *What are you going to do?*

Shut up for hell's sake! Maybe it'll be better if Mom is sober and drug-free when they catch up with us. You ever think of that? She argued more with the other voice. Driving off would give the cops time to investigate the death—the murder. Then they would see it was self-defense. With the CSI specialists and technology today, they would figure it out. *By that point, maybe—*

Maybe what?

Maybe... I don't know.

What are you afraid of?

Just shut up. I don't want to talk right now.

Cars blew by them in the other lane. Liberty was only driving thirty miles per hour. A red vehicle started passing their van then slowed. Inside, a middle-aged man and his wife craned their heads to look at her. Liberty glimpsed their white faces illuminated by dashboard lights, their eyes wide with questions.

They know, don't they? She wondered if they would call the cops and tell them they saw a juvie driving a van. Running away from something.

Her white knuckles clenched the wheel, and the gas pedal felt awkward. She kept her speed low, and cars continued to pass.

Well, you certainly won't get pulled over for speeding. Nice getaway, Liberty.

Please just shut up.

Did you really kill that man? Did you see all the blood? Did you hear him gurgle? Did you see his eyes asking for help?

I didn't kill him. He killed himself.

Is that what they'll think? Is that what you really think?

Liberty sighed. *I don't know! Leave me alone!*

She couldn't shut off the voice in her head, so she turned the radio on to distract herself. She eased up on the gas then braked slowly as she neared a red stoplight. At the last moment, she pressed the brake too hard, and JJ lurched forward out of her kinked position. She shook her head, eyes rolling, lips spread in a sly smile, and went back out.

Liberty glanced in the rearview mirror. The flashing lights weren't moving anymore. They'd gathered at the trailer park. The police would soon find out they weren't there—that they'd run.

The neighbors would point out, "Saw them leave in their green van. Dodge, I think. They went that way."

The light turned green. She pressed on the gas and shot them into the intersection. Liberty jerked the wheel to the right and turned. She heard the wheels screech. JJ's body shifted onto Liberty, and she shoved her mother back to the opposite side.

"Mom! Come on!"

Are you angry?

What do you think?

She glared at her mom.

LIBERTY DROVE INTO the parking lot of a Sleep Inn motel on the other side of town. If she could reserve a room without a credit card and use a fake name, there was a dark space around the back of the motel she could hide the van.

They wouldn't rent the room to her, so she had to drag her mom in. JJ stayed sober enough to nod and agree to the terms. Liberty told the attendant that her mom was extremely tired. She'd just taken some cold medicine that was knocking her out. Ten minutes later, she had a room key. Liberty moved the van around back then began to transport her mother and suitcase to the room.

She turned the key and pushed the door in, which released a trapped, musky smell disguised with cleaning product remnants. The light inside illuminated the contents with a dull-yellow glow. The room appeared clean, and that was good enough for her. She knew better than to search too hard for grossness. It would only send her heebie-jee-bies into overtime.

CHAPTER EIGHT

Detective Clay Baxter stepped out of his vehicle and looked at the scene in front of the trailer home. He'd received the call, sped from his house, and arrived in under ten minutes. Two police officers were on the front lawn, speaking with a short lady in a robe. She appeared to be in her late seventies. Several groups of curious people stepped cautiously out of their homes. One man was wearing nothing but jogging pants and stared at the two officers. Then, as he scratched his bare belly, his attention turned to Clay. Clay eyed him for only a moment before crossing the street to the officers.

One of the officers approached Clay. "Detective Baxter." The officer nodded and gave him a smile.

"Parsons," Clay said. "Were you first on scene?"

"Yes. Officer Bell and me. We got called out to a domestic disturbance complaint. Several calls came in from neighbors hearing screams and what sounded like a fight coming from this house. The neighbor here"—he hooked a thumb at the short old lady, who gave Clay a smile and waved her hand—"says she knows the people who live here. A mother and her daughter. She saw them drive away, like a bat outta hell, in a green van."

"Did you see which way they headed?" Clay asked the lady, and she nodded.

"Thatta way." She pointed to the west.

"I already called it in," Parsons said. "Units are combing the streets for the van."

"Well done." Clay nodded and patted Parsons on the shoulder.

"Whatever happened," Parson said, then his voice turned grim, "left a man dead. The victim's inside."

Clay stepped past the officer and entered the ominous trailer. The silent home screamed terror, violence, and murder. It would be forever marked with the ghosts that bore witness to that night.

As required to enter the scene, Clay placed plastic covers over his shoes and latex gloves on his hands. He stood a foot inside the entrance and surveyed the front room. The mobile home was aged with use and abuse. The shag carpet was dark and matted along the higher trafficked areas. Wood-paneled walls from the seventies lined the home. Several pictures hung on them, and more rested on shelves with trinkets. He stepped up to an eight-by-ten photograph that sat on a shelf. A young girl with light-brown hair, dark-chocolate eyes, full cheeks, a button nose, and a wide, radiant smile stared at him. He guessed the girl's age in the picture to be around ten years old. Although the face and smile appeared happy, Clay saw a hint of tragedy and sadness in her eyes.

He stepped farther into the room, careful not to bump anything out of its position, and his shoes crunched glass. Items scattered the ground, some broken and others whole. The TV in the far corner sat tilted where it had fallen.

He approached the victim. The body lay facedown on the coffee table. His left hand hung off the table and rested on the crimson-stained carpet, which was already drying in spots. Clay crouched and inspected the apparent cause of death lodged in the man's throat.

He stood up and walked the rest of the room, taking in every detail. He stopped and turned back to face the coffee table, where the victim's feet and legs dangled. He studied the area, trying to determine the cause of his fall. Perhaps he had been thrown, been tripped by someone, or had accidentally fallen during a fight. He looked at the ground and saw an iron skillet. Clay raised an eyebrow.

There were more pictures on the end table. In an older one of a mother and daughter, bushy trees lined the background. They appeared to be in the mountains somewhere, perhaps camping. The mom was in jeans and a blouse, and the young girl, around eight years old, held her mother's hand and pulled a funny face. The mom's tongue stuck out, too, and she crossed her eyes.

Another eight-by-ten picture sat next to it. A school picture of the girl. She was older in that image. Her cheeks were thinner, and she appeared mature and confident. She looked closer to thirteen. Clay studied her dark-brown eyes and matching hair and imprinted them in his memory.

"C-Bax!" his partner, Jim Calloway, called as he entered the house.

The nickname was taken from Clay's email address, cbaxter@SW-PD.gov. Calloway had shortened it. He was one of those guys who gave everyone a nickname. He had moved from the East Coast to Stillwater, Oklahoma, five years ago. Two years later, he'd been assigned to Clay.

"You got this mystery solved yet?"

Clay turned to him and rolled his eyes. "Right. We just have to catch our runaways. Then we can get to the bottom of this."

Calloway walked over to him and pointed at the dead body. "Who's the guy lying down on the job?"

"That's a boyfriend, I'm guessing. According to the neighbor, a mother and daughter live here. They're nowhere to be seen. A neighbor says she saw them both drive off, heading west. We'll catch up with them."

A dark piece of metal caught Clay's eye, and he stepped around Calloway toward an overstuffed magazine rack against the wall. Something stuck out from beneath it. As he got closer, he recognized the butt of a gun.

Clay crouched to look at it. "We have a gun. Nine-millimeter semi."

"Was the guy shot?"

"Don't think so. There's blood and a good sized lump on the back of his head, and of course, the blade in his throat, but I don't see a gunshot." Clay stood up and surveyed the room again. "There was definitely a fight, maybe over the gun. Probably knocked free and slid under here."

The two continued to carefully inspect each room of the home. Clay uncovered several used needles in both the bathroom and in the master bedroom. He turned to Calloway, holding one of the needles and shaking his head.

"The mother's got a drug problem. Heroin from what I can tell."

"What about the daughter?"

Clay stepped into the daughter's bedroom.

"No. Her room is clean. Bed is made, nothing on the floor, clothes folded neatly in her dresser," Clay said as he opened drawers and inspected their contents. "It's like she's the complete opposite of her mom, whose room is a pigsty."

Clay found a book inside her top drawer with the title *My Diary* on the cover. He opened it, read through several pages, and was surprised to find poems. He stopped on one.

"Your Secret Life"

I see you changing right before my eyes, why all the secrets & lies?
You try to hide this secret life from me, but I see it all...
You think these drugs will make you happy or take away the pain?
They WON'T. Instead, they will destroy you, they will destroy us...
Clay flipped through a couple more pages and read another that caught his eye.

"Love & Hate"

You bring me so much love yet so much hate...
How can I love you & hate you all at the same time?
Easy... DRUGS!!!

A flash from Clay's childhood struck him, and memories sank like ships in his stomach. He read one more.

"Love Me"

As I find you passed out on the couch, I am not sure if
You're dead or alive, as you're so high I can't wake you...

What the HELL is wrong with you?

How can you do this to yourself, to me, to us?

Why can't you just love me more than the drugs?

"Find anything in there?" Calloway asked, and Clay raised his eyebrows.

"A teenager's angry emotions. Just another sad story."

CHAPTER NINE

*A*re you okay?

Liberty's conscience spoke to her. Unlike the other voices in her head, her conscience spoke to her in a soothing, comforting tone. Most of the time, it helped. But not that day. Nothing cooled her nerves. Her anger, fear, and anxiety were at an all-time high. She faced a whole different world than two hours ago, and it was uncharted territory.

Are you okay?

She wanted to wring that voice's neck and beat it against the wall.

Liberty placed a cold, damp washcloth on her mother's right temple while she lay on the bed. Liberty had already stripped it of the comforter and thrown it in the corner of the room. *The hotel rarely washes those.* Her hands still shook from the shock of the attack. Bruises were already forming on her mom. She was reminded of older days with abusive boyfriends like Pete.

Eyes closed, JJ groaned. There was an open wound on her temple. It didn't bleed, but it needed cleaning, and it was going to sting like a bitch.

"Thank you, Lib." She pulled her eyelids open and smiled.

Liberty's face hardened, and she looked away without responding.

As if sensing Liberty's anger, JJ apologized. "I'm so sorry, sweetie." She reached a hand up to stroke her cheek, but Liberty pulled away.

"He was your drug dealer, wasn't he?" Her voice was cold.

In a low, shameful voice, JJ said, "Yes."

"He came to kill you. Maybe me too. *Why?*"

"I don't know. Honestly, I don't."

"He said you stole his money, and Duke beat him up. Don't bull-shit me, Mom."

"I'm not. I really *don't* know," she pleaded. Her eyes held honesty. "I tried callin' Jimmy a hundred times, but he's not answering. If he really did this..." She looked away and shook her head.

Liberty crossed the room and plopped into a chair, hung her head, then closed her eyes.

"Liberty?"

"Better get some sleep, Mom."

"But I—"

"I don't want to talk right now. Just get some rest." Her tone was deep and cutting.

The drug dealer's face kept flashing through Liberty's mind, every detail etched in. The dark bangs dangling over his forehead, the wild eyes, acne scars and the bruises on his cheeks, and the dripping blood that screamed to be wiped away from his mouth. He reeked of a stench that could only be described as a mix between stale cigarettes, sweat, and the smell of fried food. The stench would never go away from her senses. Neither would the copper stink of blood. It would always be at-tached to that night's memory. Just like his wide, yellow-toothed grin. When his face was pressed close to hers before he threw her, she could see remnants of bread stuck between his teeth. They were the strangest of details, but they continued to spin in her head.

The glimmer of steel from his knife was sharp in her mind, as was his knee smashing into the side of her mom's head. But the worst image of all, and the one she tried to stuff away but couldn't, was his face as he choked on the blood, quarts of it flooding his mouth and wound. His eyes had pleaded for help, but she hadn't given any.

Liberty didn't feel the tears until they dripped onto her hands. She tried her best but couldn't hold back the sobs.

What's going to happen now?

I don't know.

The police are going to come. They'll find you.

I know.

You shouldn't run.

I gotta run.

You could call your aunt. She's always been good to you. She'll help you.

I know she would. I also know she'd immediately take custody of me and not try to help my mom. Mom needs to get better. Once she sobers up, she can help me figure this out. Maybe I can finally convince her to get help.

Rehab? You know she won't go.

I have to try.

The police are going to charge her with murder. Maybe you too.

We didn't kill him! He fell. It was an accident. Besides, he was trying to kill us.

A heroin addict and her angsty thirteen-year-old daughter? They won't bother to find the truth.

Shut up! Who the hell are you anyway? Aren't you supposed to be helping me? Supporting me?

I'm sorry. Are you okay?

Liberty sighed and shut the voice out.

She opened her eyes and stared at the door then the window. Lights from the red vacancy sign of the hotel kept blinking through the curtains. She heard the rumble of a car driving by then quieting as it got farther away, and silence rent the night again. For a moment, the blinking light from the sign tricked her into thinking the cops had shown up, and any second, they would be pounding against the door. When exhaustion finally overwhelmed the tension, Liberty got scattered moments of sleep.

At some point, she heard her mother walk into the bathroom and click the light on. She didn't come out for over twenty minutes. Liberty's hope for sobriety was shot.

CHAPTER TEN

Jon Grinder stared out at the bleak gray sky from the third-story apartment window with his one good eye. When asked about his other eye, he told the tale of a flying piece of metal from an IED explosion during his third Iraqi tour. He lied, of course, too ashamed to tell the truth. His left socket was lower than the right, eyelid half-shut and pupil unmoving and dead. It looked not unlike a sunny-side up egg sliding off the side of his face. A jagged scar ran straight up to his scalp from his socket, and a smaller one zigzagged to his left temple.

He was an average-sized man, just shy of six feet tall, with well-groomed brown hair and one dark-chocolate eye. His dead eye was ice blue. Fully clothed, he appeared generally fit, but once his torso and arms were bare, the definition of his biceps and abs stood out.

He turned back to the sobbing man tied to a chair. The man's face was a wreck of bruises and blood. His chair sat on top of a large plastic painter's cloth. Jon had prepared for a mess.

"I really don't know why I'm here," the man cried. "What do you want with me?"

"It's not what *I* want. It's what *he* wants." Jon sat down in a chair across from him.

"Who?"

"The man who hired me. *Your* employer. Or I should say former employer. This is officially your termination of employment."

"What? Why? I don't get it."

"Play stupid all you want. It's not going to help," Jon said coolly. He turned to the table next to him, where a bulky black cloth sat. It looked like a large Tootsie Roll. He unrolled the cloth, revealing several shiny bladed objects. Mostly knives of various sizes, but there were other specialty items sheathed inside, such as a corkscrew and pliers. He withdrew an eight-inch-long nickel-plated knitting needle.

"Do you like needles, Mr. Lathimer?"

Lathimer writhed in his chair, and his chest pumped up and down quickly. "You're *him*, aren't you? The one they call Grinder. I've heard about you."

Jon held the needle in front of his face, inspecting it. He didn't answer.

"I've heard how you got your name. Your methods, I mean. Such as putting men's hands in meat grinders."

Jon shrugged. "Not just men's. Anyone's really. You'd be surprised how many times I've not had to go through with it. When I'm questioning a person, they tend to squeal before their fingertips touch the rotating blades."

"That's me." Face slick with sweat, Lathimer panted. Staring at the needle with bulging eyes, he said, "I'll tell you anything. Whatever you need to know. No need for torture."

Jon turned to the man. "Who said I'm questioning you?"

Lathimer gulped.

"I said this was a termination meeting. My client had specific requests as to how it's to be done. And he's a very *sick* man." Jon shook his head slowly and twirled the long needle. It caught the kitchen light and gleamed.

Jon scooted his chair closer to the man then leaned over until they were face-to-face. At the sight of the needle, Lathimer pulled his head back as far as it could go, but Jon grabbed the man's right ear and a handful of his hair in one hand to hold his head in place. He pointed the needle like a surgeon toward Lathimer's right eye, preparing to puncture the pupil. He inched it close enough to touch. Lathimer fought hard to escape, twisting and turning, but Jon held him tight.

"I lost an eye once. Ask me if it hurt," Jon said.

"Please, dear God, help me. Don't do this. You don't have to do this. I can disappear. I'll return the money. With *interest*."

"When I lost my eye," Jon continued, "it hurt like *hell*. But it happened quick. Unfortunately, this won't be quick. I'll be inserting it slowly."

Lathimer screamed, and he struggled to get free. Jon let go of Lathimer's hair and watched as his victim fell backward and slammed onto the floor. Jon jumped on top of him and pressed his knees against Lathimer's shoulders, pinning him. He grabbed the man's hair again in one fist and held his head down. He descended the needle into his eye. Lathimer let loose his bladder, wetting himself, and he screamed incessantly until Jon was through.

Jon rose to his feet as Lathimer' s body convulsed from the brain hemorrhage. Blood and milky fluids ran from his socket and spread across the plastic liner on the floor.

Jon's cell phone vibrated in his front pocket, and he withdrew it in his latex-covered hand. CX614999 flashed across the screen, and that was all. It was code for another job, and it was specific to a client. He responded with a PO box number—one of many he had throughout the state—deleted the message, then slid the phone back into his front pocket.

He walked back to the small dining table then picked up the nine-millimeter semiautomatic pistol lying on top of it. The gun had a sound suppressor attached, and as he passed by the man still jerking on the floor, he shot him twice in the forehead with two muted pops from his gun.

Jon moved through the apartment, inspecting, and cleaning any type of evidence that would link him to the execution. It paid to remain clean-cut and well-groomed. Less chance of leaving a stray hair. Once he felt confident of his cleaning, he left the apartment, removed his latex gloves, and sealed them in a plastic storage bag. He would dispose of them in another location. He slid into the driver's side of his black Dodge Ram truck and drove across town to the post office.

He walked the hall of PO boxes until he reached his at the end. He unlocked it and was not surprised to see a new package. His client had followed Jon's instructions exactly as he had two times before. That would mark the third hit Jon had done for Rick Pines. He was a prominent drug dealer in Oklahoma, and since a heroin epidemic smothered the state currently, Pines's business thrived.

He opened the bulging envelope and grinned at the stack of cash inside. There was a note with two names typed out. Jemma Justice and Liberty Justice. Below their names it read And boyfriend.

Few things in life stunned Jon anymore. A prepared man wasn't easily shocked, but these two names stopped his heart. He quickly closed the envelope and looked around as if being watched. An older lady passed him with a slight smile, and Jon returned the salutation.

Heart racing and feeling claustrophobic, Jon hurried out of the post office to breathe the air in deeply. "Jemma Justice?" He chuckled at the irony. "*JJ?* And little *Libby?*"

He entered his truck, started the engine, and let the AC envelop him as his thoughts swam. JJ was a woman from his past. An ex-girlfriend. Several years ago, before serving in the war, he'd lived with her for a few months. He'd left her to serve his country in Iraq. After his third tour, he'd returned to her, and they'd struck up a relationship again. But she had had a daughter while he'd been gone, and nothing was the same as it had been before.

For all of the pain he'd suffered at Jemma's hands, fate had rewarded him with that piece of paper. He looked at it again in disbelief. *What did you do?*

He glanced at his watch. It was ten minutes before noon. He drove onto Main Street and looked for a pub. He pulled over at the first bar he found and entered.

His eyes had to adjust from the contrast of bright daylight to the dismal darkness of the tavern. He approached the bar and sat down on a stool.

"What can I get ya, pal?" a large bald man with a mustache asked from behind the counter.

"Whatever's on tap," Jon said in a gravelly voice. When the bartender filled his glass with beer, Jon handed him a five-dollar bill and told him to keep the change.

He turned to the large-screen TV mounted from the ceiling on the other side of the room. The twelve o'clock news was starting, and Jemma made the headline story. Jon watched intently as the anchor woman described the terrible scene from the night before that had left one man dead. The victim's name was Billy Ray Pines. *Now it makes sense.* Jon had met Rick Pines's brother a couple of times. He got the sense that Billy Ray was a wild card, a low life, and never could live up to the status of his older brother.

A picture of Jemma popped up on the screen. It was an old mug shot, and Jemma's face was haggard, her eyes and cheeks sunken in. Then they posted a headshot of her daughter.

"You've grown up, Libby," he muttered to himself.

He thought of the last day he'd seen them and how it had all ended, and he clenched his teeth in anger. Jon would relish the opportunity to wipe Jemma from the face of this earth. The universe had rewarded him. Liberty was just a rug rat, and he wouldn't bat an eye to kill her either. He'd done worse.

The anchorwoman stated that they were both still missing and, if anyone had any information, to please contact the local police department and not to approach them. They were suspected to be armed and dangerous.

Jon gulped down the last of his beer, thanked the bartender, then left.

CHAPTER ELEVEN

Liberty sat in a chair squeezed between the bed and wall, staring at the motel door across from her. It was closed and silent. Light from the day leaked through its edges. She waited for the police to pound on the door, but no one came the entire night. They'd gotten away. *For now.* She felt a glimmer of security and a delusional belief that if they stayed holed up in that room and never left, they would be safe. In the back of her mind, she knew that was a false hope.

Her phone vibrated. She looked at the text that came across. It was Amanda. *WTF??? Cops just left my house! What's going on?*

Fear pinched her heart. She texted back. *What did you tell them?*

She waited for a few seconds before Amanda responded.

Nothing. I don't know anything. They asked if you been in contact with me. I said no.

Amanda wasn't the best at grammar when it came to texting, and it bothered Liberty, who had been labeled a Grammar Nazi. It was the writer in her, but she didn't try to correct her friend.

Cop seemed nice, Amanda texted. *Not an asshole like some. R U in trouble???*

Maybe, she replied. *I am on the run. You'll probably see it on the news. I better not talk about it. Just in case.*

Right. I got your back.

Liberty typed the next message then reread it. *Whatever you do hear on the news or from the cops, just know it's not true. It's not the way it happened.*

She sent the text and waited. There was a long pause before she got a reply. She wondered if the cops were with Amanda right then. *What if they can trace the text? Can they do that?* She didn't know. She wanted to turn the TV on several times, but she was too afraid of what she would find. She wasn't ready to see their house on the news and medics wheeling a dead, covered body away from it. Meanwhile, a picture of her and her mom would be on the top right of the screen as fugitives. *If you see these people or have any knowledge pertaining to this case, please call your local police or 911 immediately. Do not engage.*

Her phone vibrated. It was Amanda again. *HOLY SHIT LIB! A guy was killed in your house?*

Are you watching the news?

No I just googled it. Have somethin to do with your mom?

Liberty typed then retyped her next message. *I can't say. Better not.*

Right. I still got your back.

Thanks.

After a break, Amanda texted, *I think they have your number.*

My phone number?

Yes.

How do they have that?

There was a delay before Amanda's next reply.

I might have kind have gave it to them. He said I needed to comply. Sorrrrry

"Shit," Liberty muttered. She was angry with Amanda, but it went away quickly. It wasn't her fault. She'd only done what she'd had to.

Just don't answer it when they call. They can't do anything with it, Amanda texted.

Can they trace me with my number? Use my phone service to GPS me or something?

There was a short pause.

No. Pretty sure they can't do that. Violatin of your rights. My cousin had an issue with her ex trying to find her. He's the abusive basterd I told you about. Tried calling Sprint to track her down. They wouldnt give him anything. Pretty sure its same for you.

I hope so.

Just be sure your location is turned off.

Good thinking. Liberty opened the settings on her phone, clicked on Cellular, and found that her location was already off. She let out a sigh of relief.

Lib I don't know what all happened but I dont think its a good idea to run from cops. If you didnt do it you shouldn't be scared. They catch u eventually.

I know, Liberty finally returned the text after processing her thoughts for a moment. *I'm just biding my time. There are some things I have to figure out first. I'm not going to run forever.*

I know this has somethin to do with your mom, Amanda wrote. *You don't have to say. But that bitch has been using you for too long. Its not right Lib. Don't go down wit her. This is all her. Know you wouldnt have anything to do with this.*

Fire pulsed in Liberty's belly as she read the word *bitch.* She had previously told Amanda a lot about her mom—all the problems, the many men in and out of her life, and the mounds of hell she'd put Liberty through. There'd been days she'd been livid toward her mom and had expressed them to Amanda with some real hate and ugly words. But it was one thing if Liberty said them. Hearing them from her friend was another thing entirely. She knew it was hypocritical, but there it was.

DON'T call her that. Please. I know what it must look like. Liberty stopped typing as tears burst from her eyes and ran down. *But she is still my mom.*

I know. I'm sorry. Didn't mean to call her that. Just upset.

Me too. My mom is sick. She's the worst she's ever been. She needs help. I just want to get her help. You know?

I know. You poor thing. Is there anything I can do?

More tears came. *I know you don't believe in God. You've told me before several times, and I understand because you've been through a lot. But just in case there is a God, can you please pray for me?*

If there is a God, I don't know why he's letting you go through all a this, Amanda wrote. *Thats just my thoughts. But yes, I'll pray for you. Only cause you asked. I don't know how though.*

Just kneel and speak from your heart. He'll listen. I know. Pray for my mom too. Okay?

Liberty thought of that violent Christmas Eve when JJ's boyfriend, Pete, had tried to enter her bedroom to give her the beating of her life. She'd believed they were done for, but Liberty had prayed to God. She'd asked for help and had received it.

You got it, Amanda texted. *Prayers for you and your mom comin up.*

Thank you.

Be careful girl okay? Don't do anything stupid. You're smart so probably wont.

Okay.

I love you.

Liberty wiped tears from her cheeks. *Love you too.*

The text conversation was over. Although the room had been silent before, the quiet inside weighed heavier then. Liberty could hear Amanda's voice through the words written on the screen, gruff and scratchy with attitude but soft when it needed to be.

Liberty clicked the screen off and looked down at the phone. Instead of a knock at the door, she feared her phone buzzing with a cop on the other end. More anxiety.

She thought of her mom. She hoped she would wake up sober, even for a moment, before shooting up again so Liberty could have a sane conversation with her about their dilemma and what to do. In all the research Liberty had done online, the professionals and past survivors talked about having to hit rock bottom before choosing to get help. They'd already faced death, killed someone, then run from the cops.

Liberty didn't think JJ could hit lower than that, but it was still too much to hope for.

"That you, Liberty?" Her mother's words were garbled as if she had a mouthful of marbles.

JJ shuffled in bed, hair splayed out about her pillow. The time on Liberty's phone read 11:12 a.m. The sound of her mother's voice triggered resentment, and anger festered in her belly. She couldn't help it.

"Liberty?"

"Yes, Mom," she said with a bothered tone.

She turned, and JJ sat up straight in bed with a frantic look on her face.

"We gotta move!" JJ stood up then rushed to the bathroom. "Hurry and get ready, Lib!"

"Wait, Mom! We have to talk."

"I know, honey, and we will." She pulled her toothbrush and paste from their travel case and prepared to brush. "We gotta make a stop first. Then, we'll talk."

"A stop? Where?" Panic exploded in her chest. *What is she thinking? Does she have errands to run?* If they left the room and drove somewhere where they could be seen, they could be caught. She wasn't ready for that. "We have to make a plan."

"I know." She paused her brushing. "We will. I promise."

Liberty did like her mom's energy, and she appeared lucid. It was promising.

TWENTY MINUTES LATER, they were inside the van hauling down Main. JJ drove.

"Don't go too fast, Mom."

"I'm not. Five over, that's it."

"In light of circumstances, you might want to drive the exact speed limit or a little under."

"Let me do the driving, Lib. I know what I'm doin'."

"Where are we going?" Perplexed, Liberty studied the stores and streets they passed and tried to figure out their destination.

"I'm stopping in at work. Gotta pick up my paycheck. If you haven't noticed, we're out of funds."

"*Work?*" Liberty's jaw dropped. "Are you insane? That's the first place the cops will be."

"I'm not stupid. I know they're probably scopin' the place out, waitin' for us to show. I ain't goin' in there. Bobbi is goin' to bring my check out to me."

"Bobbi can't get your check. Mr. Handlin is not going to give it to her. Haven't we tried this before?"

"Bobbi won't be askin'. She'll just take it. What Mr. Handlin doesn't know won't hurt him. It's my check, and I have every right to get it."

Liberty sighed and shook her head in disbelief. JJ's hands trembled, and her body shook with tiny convulsions. Liberty had seen it before. Her body was out of its poison, and it hungered for more—*needed* more.

JJ dialed a number on her phone with one hand while the other kept hold of the wheel. "Bobbi? It's JJ."

"JJ? What the hell? I saw the news!" JJ had her on speaker phone, and as loud as Bobbi was, Liberty could hear every word.

"I know. It's a total shit show. Tell you 'bout it later. I need your help. Can you get me my check?"

"Your check? I don't know, honey. Handlin's not goin' to be good about that."

"I don't want you to ask him. Just go up to the office when he's not there. Open the tin box on his desk. It's in there. That's where he keeps all of 'em."

"I'll get in trouble."

"No, you won't." JJ brought the phone closer to her mouth and enunciated her words as if coaxing her friend. "Don't get caught, an' you'll be fine."

"He'll know when he comes back and notices your check is gone. He'll think I did it."

"He won't. You didn't do it. Tell him you saw me sneak in. Real quick like and I was out. You didn't know what I was doin'. He'll think it was me."

"Then you'll be in trouble."

"What for? That check is mine. I worked for it. It belongs to me." Her face was enraged as if she'd been wronged.

Liberty listened while looking out the front and side windows of the van for any police cars. It was so bright outside, so open. They were an easy target.

"What kinda trouble you in?" Bobbi asked. "Did you *kill* that man?"

"No. Hell no. He slipped and fell. It was an accident. He was tryin' to kill me and my daughter."

"Mom, I don't know that you should be telling anyone," Liberty whispered to her, but JJ waved her off.

"I don't know. I'm not sure I can do this." Bobbi's voice trembled.

"Yes, you can. I need this. I need this real bad." The desperation in JJ's voice was tangible. "Can you do it for me? Please?"

"I'll try."

"Thank you, Bobbi! That's all I ask. Just try." She hung up and set the phone down.

Cash burned in Liberty's right pocket, approximately fifty dollars, but she kept that knowledge to herself. They were going to need it, and she would be damned before she used it for her mom's heroin.

Moments later, they pulled into the parking lot at the Happy Service.

"Mom! Cop car! Up there!" Liberty pointed across the lot.

A police vehicle was parked near the entrance. At their distance, they couldn't tell if anyone was in it or not.

"*Dammit!*" JJ cranked the wheel.

Tires squealed slightly as the van turned sharply, and JJ headed in the opposite direction. She drove out of the lot, up the street, and into the back entrance of the parking lot to the rear of the store. JJ drove along the loading dock and stopped. JJ was breathing as if she'd run a marathon. She texted Bobbi, waited a moment, then turned to Liberty.

"Really?" Liberty asked at her mother's expectant look.

JJ glared. "We have to get money."

"We have another night prepaid at the motel. Plenty of food for a few days. I even brought our camping gear. We could wait until the smoke clears a bit and come back when no cops are watching the store."

"Liberty, I'm not saying it again." She gave her daughter a stern don't-mess-with-me look. "We need the money."

They waited for five long minutes in silence before Liberty broke it. "We *need* to talk."

"Dammit, Lib, I know. I said we will."

"We could now."

"Now? You want to talk now? Go ahead." JJ's eyes were wild. "We have two minutes before Bobbi's going to shoot out that door and run my check to me, and we have a cop in front of the store ready to bust us. But let's have a conversation."

JJ's sarcasm cut Liberty. She shook her head in disgust and turned to stare out the window.

"Come on, Bobbi, where the hell are ya?" JJ mumbled.

Liberty heard JJ typing out a text, and the phone chimed as it was sent. Still nothing. Finally, JJ's phone dinged a response. Liberty scanned the text conversation as JJ held the phone in her lap.

I can't get it. He's still in there.

Handlin?

Yes. He's putting next week's schedule together, and the tin box is right next to him.

JJ pounded the dashboard with a fist. "The damn pussy is too scared to get my check." JJ moaned before texting Bobbi back. *Just ask him for it then. He's got to give it to you.*

You sure you want me to? He's not going to do it. I know.

Just try. I really need that check.

"He's not going to give it to you," Liberty said.

"I know!" She ran a nervous hand through her sweaty scalp. "Gotta try though."

Minutes went by, then finally Bobbi sent a text. *I got it! I got your check!*

He gave it to you?

A long pause. *Yes.*

JJ grinned at Liberty. "She's bringing it! She asked him for it, and the son of a bitch gave it to her. Can you believe it?"

"No." Liberty shook her head. She had a sinking feeling. "I don't believe it, and neither should you."

"What?"

"Why would Mr. Handlin give her your check?"

"Because it's mine. I'm owed a paycheck!" JJ bellowed. "He knows he can't keep it from me!"

"Has he ever done this for you before?"

"No. He's always a prick about it. Won't let me get my check till five p.m. on payday, and he won't let anybody else pick it up for me."

"I know. But today he does? You're a fugitive on the run for murder, and he decides today's the one day in years he'll allow someone else to pick up your check?"

JJ furrowed her brow. "What are you saying?"

"I'm saying there's a cop out front. This is a trap. He's allowing her to pick it up for you because when she comes out with your check, she won't be alone. The cop will be with her."

"That *bitch*." JJ's lips twisted into a snarl.

"We gotta get outta here."

The door to the outside stairs opened, and they snapped their heads up in anticipation. It stood open halfway. No one could be seen. JJ's foot rested above the gas pedal, ready to punch it. Shadows shifted behind the door. Then a woman's figure appeared. When they could make out the curly shape of her hair in the silhouette, JJ turned to Liberty.

"See, it *is* Bobbi!" JJ gripped the steering wheel.

Bobbi stepped out with check in hand. She waved at JJ, but her face was pale and clenched with anxiety, eyebrows upturned as though she might cry at any moment. A glint of steel flashed behind her, then Liberty saw the tall figure. The officer stepped out into the light. He quickly ducked back inside as if he'd realized his mistake.

"The bitch tried to bait me." JJ glared at Bobbi. "They actually thought I'd come to the door? Idiots!"

Bobbi pulled an apologetic face and mouthed, "I'm sorry."

JJ slammed the gear shift into drive and sped out of there.

The officer bolted down the stairs. In the rearview mirror, Liberty saw him running after them and speaking into the radio attached to his shirt, probably calling for backup.

JJ careened around the corner with a squeal of tires. The van halted inches away from a police car, which also screeched to a stop. Liberty realized that the cop running had been talking to his buddy in the car to cut them off.

JJ narrowed her eyes, pursed her lips, and yanked the gear into reverse. The van shot backward several feet before JJ spun the wheel with a stuntman's skill and tore off in the opposite direction.

Liberty held on tight as her mother accelerated and headed straight for the other policeman. His feet were spread, and his hands were motioning for them to stop.

"Gonna play chicken with me?" JJ didn't slow down or turn, and the cop jumped out of the way before getting squashed.

"*Mom!*" Liberty shouted.

The cop car was on their rear like glue, and Liberty couldn't see how they would lose him. She gawked at her mother, who seemed so amped with adrenalin she practically vibrated. The van tipped almost on two wheels as JJ turned a sharp corner around the building and headed for the road.

JJ didn't look left or right as she flew through an intersection. By sheer luck, no one got in their way. Liberty twisted to look behind them, and the cop was still on their tail. He couldn't have been more than ten feet away. The road wound through a neighborhood, and JJ ran through two four-way stops. The next intersection was a stoplight that had just turned red for them. It was Main Street, and cars were zipping along. The crossing traffic began to drive through a green light, and Liberty figured that was that. They couldn't drive through a line of crossing traffic. They would have to stop.

Behind them, the cop's siren was blaring, and his lights were flashing. A couple of cars seemed to hesitate due to the oncoming officer.

"You gotta stop, Mom. *Mom.*"

She didn't slow down. It was as if JJ were leaving it all to chance, hoping they would make it through without getting hit or killed.

Liberty held her breath, wanting to shut her eyes but couldn't. She saw a blur of colors as vehicles sped through the intersection, and before she knew it, their van was in the center of it. Horns honked, and tires squealed. Liberty watched in horror as the bumper of a gray Honda came within inches of her door, but the car turned. Blue smoke escaped from beneath its screeching tires as the driver braked and slid to a stop.

We made it! They crossed to the other side with not so much as a scratch. Liberty looked behind them. The cop approached the intersection more carefully than her mother had. There was a growing cluster of cars in the middle where people were stopping. The policeman suddenly gunned it around them. He almost got to the other side.

With the oncoming traffic, a dump truck was rocketing toward the clump of cars blocking the intersection. To avoid disaster, he turned his truck at the same moment the cop passed through. What Liberty guessed was a twenty-thousand-pound vehicle braked, but that did not stop it from slamming into the rear of the squad car.

Pieces of fiberglass and plastic exploded from the police car's back end, and it spun twice before it rolled. The high-pitched crunch of metal and glass pushed out all other sound, and the squad car slid on its top for several feet.

"Holy shiiiiiiit!" JJ howled a laugh.

"*Mom*! That cop could be hurt!"

"Whose side are you on?" JJ asked.

"Don't make me choose."

JJ turned three more times through another neighborhood before hitting a main road and heading east on it. A few minutes later, the sirens became distant enough that they were barely audible, but it didn't calm Liberty's nerves any better, and JJ wasn't slowing down.

Liberty's phone vibrated. An incoming call. She looked down at it. It read Unknown.

Cops! She was sure of it, and her body clenched. She didn't answer. She put the phone away.

CHAPTER TWELVE

Hank Bellow, Narcotics Division, marched through the precinct then plopped into a chair in front of Clay's desk. Clay looked up to see him slam a tall can of Rockstar on his desktop.

"Hey, rock star!" Hank grinned.

A pleasant smile crossed Clay's face when he saw the can. "Thanks."

Hank was an unusually tall man of almost seven feet. His size, handlebar mustache, and strong stature would intimidate any front linemen on a football field.

"You're gonna need it. Ain't no sleepin' on this job." Hank cracked open his own Rockstar and took a gulp. "So Billy Ray got knifed by one of his own customers?"

"I'm still waiting for the medical examiner's report, but I don't think it went down like that. From what I can tell, Billy Ray came to their house to kill Jemma. Maybe the daughter too. A fight ensued, and he ended up dead. Either by an accident or self-defense."

"They ran, didn't they?"

Clay nodded.

"That ain't good. Not good t'all."

"What can you tell me about Billy Ray Pines?"

"Billy Ray? He pushes drugs in this territory for his brother. Rick is the real kingpin. He's one of the heads of the Dixie Mafia, and he protects Billy Ray and this territory heavily. Brother's got a gambling problem, a drug problem, and a management problem, but they always bail him out. Blood is thick. I always figured one day he'd be their downfall."

"How do you mean?"

"They're good ol' boys. Grew up in the country, and their family is everything. Billy Ray may have been a screwup, but they are not going to let his death go unavenged. I know Rick and how he thinks. Unlike his younger brother, he's an intelligent businessman. We've been building a case against him and the Dixie Mafia for a long time. We've busted a lot of his lower-level drug dealers, but they won't rat him out."

"Because of loyalty?"

Hank shook his head. "Out of *fear*. He's learned a few things from the Sinaloa Cartel. If you rat on him, he'll kill your whole family."

"Does he work with the cartel?"

Hank widened his eyes. "No. That's the funny thing. The cartel owns Oklahoma. It's an epidemic, and we don't have the manpower to shut it down. They run drugs in, and they hold many of their dealers' families hostage in Mexico to keep them from narking 'em out. They control everything but Pines's region, and there was a big turf war until Rick brought in the Grinder."

"The Grinder?" Clay scrunched his face.

"He's a hired hitman. He's efficient and ruthless, and he tore through several of the cartel's higher-ups until they backed off. You ever see *The Terminator*?"

"Of course."

"He's like that, and he's the one you have to look out for now. Rick is going to want revenge for his brother, and he's too smart to do it himself. Most likely, he'll contract out the murder to the Grinder." Hank paused to take a big gulp from his can. "The man's a ghost, and we've been hunting him for a long time too. He doesn't leave a trace. He leaves nothin' but his reputation and name. He'll track them both down. He won't stop to sleep or eat until he gets ahold of them, and the only thing they'll be able to do is pray it's quick because this guy..." He paused, and a shade of gray crossed his face. "I've seen his victims. You don't want anyone to end up like them."

"I can't believe Rick Pines would care so much about taking out a strung-out heroin addict and her child. He's risking everything now." Clay leaned back in his chair, shrugging his arms.

"News will be on the streets fast. He'll put up a cash reward for any sighting or information."

"Then we have to get to Jemma and Liberty before his hitman does."

"Time is ticking, amigo. Anything I can do?"

"Anything and everything you can do is appreciated. You hear any reports about their whereabouts through your sources, let me know."

"She's a heroin addict. She's going to need more of it soon. She'll be hittin' somebody up. I'll keep my eyes and ears out and check my sources and let you know if something pops up."

Clay stood up to leave, but Hank stopped him.

"Clay. This is bigger than some dope whore and her kid. We have a real shot at getting this hitman and bringing down Rick Pines. I'd like my team included on this."

Hesitant, Clay wrinkled the corners of his eyes. "They're *not* bait, and I won't use them as such. And don't call her a crack whore." He gritted his teeth in distaste. "This is a mother and her child. Don't forget that. They are the victims."

"Verdict's still out on that. Dope makes you do crazy things. It could a' been she killed him in cold blood. You ever think a' that?"

"My only job right now is to bring them in safely. We'll sort out the truth and law from there."

"Clay!" Calloway called from across the room, and Clay turned. "Our girls have been spotted!"

Clay grabbed his jacket and rushed over to his partner. "Where?"

CHAPTER THIRTEEN

The van caught air as JJ flew over a small dip in the road at seventy miles an hour in a thirty-five before slamming back to the ground again. A sign ahead warned them to slow down to twenty-five for a sharp turn, but she took it at sixty and nearly flipped the van on its side.

"Geez, Mom!" Liberty held tight to the oh-shit handle in the ceiling while being thrown left and right.

"We gotta cover some distance! Cops will be all over the place!"

"Yes, and you're making us a good target."

"I'll slow down when we've put them far behind us." JJ looked in the rearview mirror. "You seen anyone yet?"

"No. Not a one."

"I think we made it out of there in the nick of time."

Liberty's phone vibrated. The caller ID read Unknown again.

"Who's calling?" Suspicion transformed JJ's face as she eyed Liberty.

"I don't know. Unknown caller."

"Don't answer. Matter a fact, throw it out the window."

"*What?*"

"They're probably tracking us right now! They got your number, baby, and they're tracing it!"

"No, they can't do that."

"How do you know?"

"Because I know. I have my GPS and tracking off. Plus, they tried to do it to a friend of mine, and they couldn't get permission from the phone company. They said it was a violation of privacy rights."

"Damn straight it is. Good for somethin', I guess."

With one hand on the wheel, JJ popped a cigarette into her mouth and lit it. Liberty sighed and rolled her window down.

JJ set the lighter down, picked her phone up, and dialed a number.

"You're gonna get us killed."

"I got one eye on the road. It's my good eye." She smiled and gave a wink.

"Where are we going?"

JJ didn't answer. She had her phone on Speaker again.

A muffled voice crackled from the other end. "Yeah?"

"Slim! How's it goin'?"

"Who the hell's this?"

"'Who the hell's this?' After all we been through? I'm hurt."

"JJ? That you?"

Her mother grinned. "The one and only."

"What can I do ya for?"

"You can do me for a hundred bucks!" She belted out laughter at her own joke, glanced at Liberty for an audience, but her ice-cold glare cut JJ's smile to nothing.

"Shit, I ain't got no hundred bucks," Slim griped.

"You know what I need."

"I ain't got nothin'. You know that. Lost my job, and I'm gettin' kicked outta this place. I'm hurtin' real bad myself. Same shit, diff'rent day. You know how it goes."

"Slim, I'm five minutes away from you."

"JJ, I ain't lyin'!"

"You owe me," JJ said. "You know you do."

"For what? I don't owe you shit."

"You don't owe me shit?" she spat. "Not from you, Slim. I helped you so many times when you were sick. I gave you shit for free! I took you in. I don't—"

The phone clicked. Slim hung up.

"Bastard!"

"Good friend," Liberty said.

"Not now, Lib. I'm in a real tough spot." JJ shook. Her haggard face and wide eyes revealed true panic and fear, and Liberty was sure it wasn't because of the cops.

Liberty knew she was hurting. She couldn't understand it. She didn't know why her mother couldn't stop shooting her body with heroin for even one day. It was beyond her comprehension and made it difficult to feel empathy.

JJ turned down another street, exiting a neighborhood and heading down a gravel road that held a handful of scattered homes. The landscape was bare, a desolate brownish gray spotted with few trees and plant material. The sky darkened as clouds rolled over the sun. They were black and full of precipitation, rising out of nowhere like billowing smoke from a fire and promising the threat of rain, thunder, lightning, and possible tornadoes.

It was an Oklahoma sky after all. Their weather could catch anyone off guard, whip through a town like the wrath of God, and humble anyone to their knees. She wondered if the storm had come to test them or punish them for their sins. Or maybe it was there to remind them there was a God, and His power was mighty, and His will would be done. *What does God have in store for us?* The question wasn't *could* He help them, but *would* He.

Distant thunder rumbled as if it were an answer from God, and Liberty wondered how to translate it. Perhaps the storm was there to help hide them from all who searched for them.

JJ parked their van in front of a small single-story rambler that looked as though it had been around since the town was developed. It must've been beaten down by storm after storm and been left wobbling on its last legs. She guessed it had been white at one time, but it was marked with so many scratches, dents, and peeled paint that it looked spotted. The roof bowed, and overgrown and unpruned trees surrounded the home. Weeds were nearly as tall as the bushes, and a detached garage leaned to one side as if too many strong winds had pushed it that way.

JJ slammed the gear into park then shut the van off. Dust from the drive curled around the vehicle, and JJ gave Liberty a shrug as if this was her last chance. They exited the vehicle and crossed to the entrance of the home.

"Why did we come here? I thought he said he didn't have anything and not to come?"

"I have to try." JJ shook her head. "You wouldn't understand."

I don't understand, she thought.

The screen door whined as JJ pulled it open and rapped on the door. The muffled sound of classic rock music came from farther in the house, but no other sound could be heard, including any movement to answer the door.

JJ knocked louder. "Slim! It's me, JJ! Open the door!"

Finally, they heard thumps and stomps approaching. Slim opened the door. He was shirtless, and Liberty rolled her eyes. He was as skinny as a skeleton wrapped in skin, and his chest bore a patch of brown hair formed into a *T*. Under his faded gray sweatpants, his feet were bare. He had long, stringy hair that ran to his shoulders, and a goatee that hadn't seen a beard trimmer in weeks. His arms were lined with red sores and scabs, but his eyes were an icy blue.

"JJ, I told you I ain't got shit. Why'd you come here?"

"I got nowhere else to go. Just let us come in for a minute."

"No, man, I can't. I got someone here."

"Slim." JJ placed a palm on his chest, pushed him back, and marched herself in. Slim stood aside and gawked at her. Liberty stood at the door, uncertain whether or not to follow.

Mockingly, Slim bowed and spread a welcoming hand. "Please, by all means." He grinned at Liberty.

The contact high was near immediate as Liberty entered a room full of smoke. The bitter sweetness of the marijuana made her stomach churn. Walking in through the front room, she had to step around a large number of items scattered on the floor. Piles of clothes, dirty dishes, pizza boxes, a motorcycle helmet, old TV remotes, an Xbox, video game cases, and crumpled fast-food bags were strewn everywhere.

She turned at the sound of gurgling. It reminded her of someone who blew bubbles into their drink with a straw. A man sat hunched over on a dilapidated couch, taking a hit from a bong. The source of the sickening smell and strange sound was answered.

The man relaxed back into the saggy sofa with slitted, bloodshot eyes and a grin. "How's it goin'?" he asked as he exhaled smoke.

"Good." She nodded. "How are you?"

"Can't complain."

I could think of a few things to complain about.

JJ walked straight into the kitchen like she owned it and opened the fridge. "Got anything to drink?"

"Got a beer, if you want one, and some lemonade."

"Lemonade?" She smirked.

"Crystal Light."

"Watching the calories? Nice. I'll pass." She slammed the fridge door.

Liberty watched them from the front room, keeping her distance but paying attention to every word.

Slim approached her mother. "JJ, what's goin' on? I heard some shit."

"Yeah? Well, don't believe any of it."

"I heard Billy Ray got jacked!"

"Billy Ray got what he deserved, let's leave it at that. He tried to kill me and my daughter. Claimed I stole from him. I've done a lot of shit in my life"—she shook a finger at him—"but you know me. I ain't never stole from nobody. At least not from the hand that feeds."

Judge Judy was playing on the TV, and the man on the couch watched the program intently. The music played from another room in the house. She recognized the song. Bad Company was playing one of their classics, "Feel Like Makin' Love."

"You like *Judge Judy*?" Liberty asked.

"Judge Judy's the bomb." He nodded. "She sees through everything. I love to watch her work these people. Watch and listen to the questions she asks. She knows just what to say to get to the truth, and she knows when they're lyin'."

Judge Judy pounded the bench in front of her with her palm. She called out to the plaintiff, whose eyes shifted to the ground while mumbling his answers, "Up here!" She grabbed his attention and motioned to her eyes with two fingers. With a stone-faced stare, she commanded the defendant to look her right in the eye the next time he talked. Then she pulled a sly smile.

The guy on the couch laughed. "She's always doin' that shit."

Liberty turned her eyes back to her mom. JJ's entire body quivered. Slim looked at her shaking hands. He gently held her wrists and looked into her eyes.

"Slim, I got 'em bad. I'm not gonna make it."

"Come into my bedroom. I'll get Jerry's bong. You can take some hits off that. Helps some."

She nodded, and Liberty watched as they disappeared into his room.

"You can take a seat," Jerry, the man on the couch, said to Liberty.

Where? Every space was occupied by something.

"Under them clothes is a chair." Jerry stood up and threw the clothes down to the ground, revealing a shaggy green recliner. He motioned for her to sit.

"Thanks. I'm fine." Liberty motioned and remained standing.

Slim entered the front room and picked up Jerry's bong and lighter. Jerry looked at him as if he'd stolen his favorite Teddy Bear.

"Don't worry. I'll bring it back."

Slim's bedroom was only a few feet from where Liberty stood, and she inched herself closer to the bedroom door so she could listen. Slim nudged the door, but it didn't close completely. Slim and JJ didn't keep their voices low, either, so Liberty was able to hear everything.

"I really don't know what I'm going to do," JJ said. "The police are after me, and who knows who else. Someone's going to want retribution for Billy Ray."

"You are in a real funk."

"I don't care what happens to me. I really don't. Get locked up, get killed, it doesn't matter. But what about *Liberty*? She doesn't deserve this. I gotta take care of her, and I can't. Slim, I just can't. I'm a shitty mother."

Tears welled up in Liberty's eyes.

"You're not a shitty mother." Slim attempted to console her.

"I am, though. I know it. I need heroin. Constantly. I need that shit, and it takes priority over everything. Including her."

The words came as no surprise, but it still made Liberty dig her nails into her hands and have to resist the urge to throw open the door to yell at her mom.

"I don't know what the hell I'm doin', and I don't know what to do next," JJ continued. "I got no money, and I got no black. You gotta help me. If I had it... then maybe I could sort shit out, you know? Right now, I can't think of anything else but getting it."

"I'd give you some if I had any. I gotta get out there and score some for myself."

"When you do, can you call me? Help me. Get some for me too."

"Yeah, of course."

Why? Liberty's shoulders sank in defeat. *Does she even remember I'm here?*

"You gotta promise me," JJ went on. "The moment you get it. Call me. Text me. Any hour. I'm not gonna make it."

Slim was silent for a moment.

"What is it?" JJ sounded desperate. "What are you hiding?"

"Not hidin' nothin'!"

"Yes, you are! What do you got?"

"I don't have any black. I promise you."

"What *do* you have?"

"I have a couple of percs," he finally said. "I can give you two, but that's it. It's all I got. It'll get you by."

"Yeah, for an hour, if I'm lucky."

"Babe, that's all I got. Better than nothin'!"

"Not much, but I'll take it. Thank you," she said.

Liberty kept her restless hands clasped together below her waist, and she shifted from leaning on one foot to the other. As she continued to block out the TV to listen to her mom and Slim, a phone chirped. The stoner's phone rested on the coffee table with a new text. On instinct, Liberty drew her eyes to the screen. Her heart dropped three floors as she saw the name Jemma on the screen followed by the words her daughter.

Jerry was in no hurry to pick it up. It chirped again from another text, and Liberty saw dollar signs on it. Chills ran through her body.

The stoner, still lying on the couch, finally picked it up and read the texts. Immediately, he sat up, and his eyes darted to Liberty. She stared back. Although no words were exchanged, she knew what it meant. Something terrible was about to happen.

Liberty heard another phone chirp from inside Slim's bedroom.

"What is it?" JJ asked.

"Ugh. Nobody," Slim grumbled.

"All right. It's been real."

"Real pain in my ass."

Liberty looked at the bedroom door as JJ's fingers appeared on the handle.

"Goin' so soon?" Slim asked.

"Yeah. I gotta," JJ said smugly.

"Why don't you hang out here for a while? We can get high."

JJ's hand paused on the door. She bit her lip as if contemplating his offer, and finally, she shook her head once. "You don't have what I need to get high. Remember?"

"I know... but we can have fun. Like we used to."

She snorted. "I got my daughter here. It ain't happenin'."

"What if I got something comin'?" he asked in a desperate tone.

"You got somethin' comin' now?" JJ's voice rose.

"Yeah."

"It was in that text?"

"*Mom!*" Liberty called to her.

Jerry stood and moved toward Liberty. "Whatcha' doin', hon?"

"I ain't your hon." She burned a hole in him with her eyes. "Mom, we gotta go. *Now!*"

"Hold on a minute, Lib," JJ said.

"Come back and watch *Judge Judy* with me," Jerry said. "You can sit on the couch. Change the channel too. Whatever you want."

"Mom! It's a *trap*! They called someone!"

JJ snapped at Slim. "You called the cops?"

"No." Slim chuckled nervously. "I wouldn't call them. You know that."

"Who'd you call? What was in that text?" she demanded, and Liberty heard a scuffle.

"No one, okay?" Slim said. "*Bitch.*"

JJ marched out of the bedroom, holding Slim's phone and reading his texts. "You son of a bitch." Her cheeks raged red. "Five hundred bucks! You sold me out for that little?"

She turned and threw the phone at him, and it bounced off his head.

Jerry grabbed Liberty's arms as JJ strode into the front room. Without hesitation, her mother ripped Jerry's fingers free from Liberty and pushed him off her. The stoner stumbled and fell to the floor.

"Let's go!" JJ charged for the door with Liberty in tow.

"JJ! Stop! I'll shoot!"

They froze. Slim stood a few feet away, pointing a revolver in shaky hands.

Before Slim could blink, JJ crossed the room, yanked the gun from his hand, then sent a right hook to his nose. The blow hit so hard that Slim twisted and fell to the carpet, blood pouring from his nostrils.

Jerry jumped to his feet and ran at JJ with gritted teeth bared. She aimed the gun and fired a shot. It rang and echoed in the small room, and the bullet hit the Xbox on the ground. The top of it exploded in smoke and sparks. The stoner froze.

"First shot's a warning. Second goes in your head. Wanna play?"

He shook his head furiously.

JJ stabbed her gaze at Slim. "Keys! Throw me the keys to your shit car!"

Slim raised his eyebrows, and his jaw dropped. "*My* car? You can't take my car!"

"*Now!*" she demanded with authority, and Slim pulled the keys from his pocket and tossed them.

Liberty caught them so her mom could keep the gun on him.

"What am I gonna do now?" Slim cried.

"Here." JJ withdrew the keys to the van from her pocket and tossed them. They dropped at Slim's feet. "You got my van now. And I'd say that's an upgrade."

JJ and Liberty exited, jumped into the 1982 Oldsmobile Cutlass Supreme, and tore away from his house.

CHAPTER FOURTEEN

Jon approached JJ's mobile home with a purpose. He didn't try to mask his intentions, didn't attempt to hide or walk carefully to the door. He marched like he was an investigator assigned to the case. It was dark from the approaching storm. Droplets splattered his shoulders, and thunder rumbled. There was a cop posted to watch the house up until a few minutes ago. Jon had waited for him to leave before advancing.

He crouched under the yellow caution tape, and the door, although locked, was easy to get into with the use of his pocketknife. He placed plastic booties over his shoes and pushed his hands into leather gloves.

Jon stepped into the stale, smoke-infested home tainted with the foul mix of coagulated blood and mustiness. It was dark inside except for a sliver of illumination as clouds parted to allow the fading sunlight in. Instead of turning on the lights, he allowed his eyes to adjust and commenced his search. The coffee table was stained with a black pool at one end that dripped down a leg to another pool on the carpet. The blood had dried in its place like paint. He moved cautiously through the mess of the house, eyeing each item, waiting for something to call out to him.

He studied each picture. There were images of JJ with a group of friends and a five-by-seven portrait with her and some man cuddling on the sofa. *A boyfriend?* He ripped the photo out of the frame, folded it, and put it in his jacket pocket. He continued to scan every item he saw into his memory so he could draw upon it later.

He stepped over to an end table where a couple of other photos sat. He picked up one of JJ holding her daughter's hand, both making funny faces. Trees and a campground lined the background, and beyond the trees was a shimmering blue lake. It took him a moment, but then he remembered the place, Lake McMurtry Park. He was sure of it. Liberty looked approximately eight years old.

"Hello, JJ. Liberty." He examined the photo through squinted eyes, taking in their appearances, then smiled. "Remember me?"

He set the photo down and pondered what their reunion would be like. He slowly walked the rest of the house.

Looks like you have a drug problem, JJ. And not just because of the dead drug dealer in your home. He laughed. When he'd dated her, she'd dabbled a bit in drugs, but nothing had gotten to this extreme. He found needles in the garbage, under the bed, and in all sorts of places throughout the house. *A bad drug problem.* He suspected she was shooting up maybe three to four times a day. Expensive. From the looks of the place, she didn't have the funds to support it. *You must be doing something to get your high. You'll always find a way.*

He walked into Liberty's room. Unlike the rest of the home, it was kept nice—clothes put in their place, bed made, and no loose junk on the floor or on top of the dressers. Posters of bands and artists including Blue October, Lorde, Evanescence, and two of Katie Perry hung on the walls. *Strange mix,* he thought. He rummaged through her dresser drawers, finding pieces of written poems, some long, some short, and some unfinished, and finally withdrew a diary from underneath clothes.

Hidden treasure, he thought, but after thumbing through it, he shrugged and tossed it to the floor. *Typical teenager.*

So where are you, JJ? Where are you and your bratty teen? He thought of Lake McMurtry. No, she wouldn't go there. Not yet. She still needed heroin. She wasn't going far from where she could score that. Hell-bent on finding black, she wouldn't care as much about hiding from the cops either. *You're bouncing all around town for it. So who's got it? Who's going to give it to you?*

He stepped outside and looked around the neighborhood. There were a couple of kids playing down the street, but that was about it. From the mobile home next to JJ's, a short woman in a robe exited and ambled to her mailbox on the street. She was hunched with age. Jon figured her to be in her eighties. She turned and straightened at the sight of him.

"Good evening." He smiled.

"Evenin', Officer," she said.

Officer? She thought he was a cop.

"I wonder if I could trouble you?" Jon said.

The woman nodded, and Jon approached.

"Have you seen other people coming and going at this house? Anyone besides Jemma and Liberty?"

"From time to time."

"Perhaps a man? Like... a boyfriend?"

"Yes. In a big-ass truck. He parks it here"—she pointed at the road in front of her house—"and I don't get mail when he does. Told him he can't park here. He *can't.*"

"Of course." Jon withdrew the folded picture he'd stolen from inside and showed it to her. "Did he look anything like this?"

Her eyes widened. "Yes, that's him, all right."

"Do you happen to know his name?"

She shook her head. "Sorry."

"How about the truck? What color is it?"

"It's a big ol' thing. One they haul things with. It's bright red. Big-Time Trucking is written on the side of it. I called them a couple a' times to tell them he can't park here. But they ignore me."

"Big-Time Trucking?" Jon said with enthusiasm. "That's very helpful. Thank you for your cooperation. You have a nice night."

"You too." She walked back into the house, appearing to have forgotten all about the mail.

His phone vibrated. It was a text from the client. A tip was reported of their whereabouts. Jon rushed to his truck. He texted a response.

Is the boyfriend with them?

No.

Tell them to keep them there. I'm on my way.

The client texted back a thumbs-up.

Jon started his engine but paused before driving away. *What to do about the boyfriend?* He couldn't be in two places at once, and yet, they both needed to be taken care of quickly. If he chased Jemma down first, he could lose the boyfriend. More likely than not, the boyfriend had the money and was using it to go underground at this moment.

He sent a message to his colleague, Lex. He was a bloodhound and could find anyone. He was the best man to put on the case, and Jon would pay him handsomely from his reward.

You open ASAP? Jon asked.

For you, yes, Lex replied.

He works for Big-Time Trucking. I don't have his name, but his rig is red. He left from Stillwater yesterday. Jon texted the info to Lex. He snapped a shot of the picture of JJ's boyfriend with his phone and sent that too. It should be more than enough info for Lex.

The package is to be delivered. He's running with cash stolen from the client, Jon texted. *Bring that as well.*

Done, Lex replied.

JON CAUGHT A SLICE of lightning to his left, and it was followed by a bellow of thunder. His truck sped down the gravel road toward the house where the tip had come from. The road was riddled with potholes and dips that rattled his truck as he drove.

A text message popped up on his phone, which was sitting on the center console, and he looked down to see what it said.

They lost them. Both the mother and daughter are gone.

Jon clenched his jaw. He brought the phone up to his mouth and, using the voice-to-text feature, said, "Tell the boys to stay put."

A few minutes later, Jon saw what had to be the house up ahead. It was the only one left on the road. Only a part of it could be seen peeking out through the overgrown brush. A green van bounced out of the driveway and turned, facing Jon. He saw two faces through the windshield with their mouths open wide and eyes even wider. Jon skidded to a stop inches short of their front bumper. They faced each other, the two men looking terrified, and Jon gritting his teeth.

The vehicle peeled out in reverse, spitting gravel, and Jon shot off like a rocket after them. They drove nose to nose in the same direction, Jon moving forward and the van driving backward. The van wavered back and forth as the driver appeared to struggle to keep it straight.

The driver of the Dodge Caravan stomped on the brakes and spun it around to face the opposite direction. The passenger's body rocked, then the van bolted forward, throwing out dirt and pebbles from under its tires and, to Jon's surprise, gaining some distance from him.

The road ahead was only getting worse. Each bump the Caravan's tires hit threatened to send it off course or tipping over. As fast as the van could go, it was no match for the Hemi engine underneath the Ram's hood. The truck bumped them from behind, and the van's driver almost lost control.

Then Jon drove alongside the van. He rolled the passenger window down, pointed his pistol, then three shots rang out. Two bullets pierced the back door, and one smashed the driver's window and whizzed past him and his passenger.

One more shot hammered and blasted out the driver's-side tire. The green van shook with a tremendous force. The driver fought with the steering wheel. Jon tapped the side of the van once more with his truck, sending it on a diagonal course to the deep ravine that ran alongside the road. The van bounced over the curb, through scrub brush, over the edge, and smashed its front end into the bottom of the dry creek.

Jon parked his vehicle at the side of the road and exited. Gun in hand, he stepped down the slope to the smoking van. The windshield was smashed, and the passenger airbag had been deployed. The man on the passenger side was holding his head, while the driver was slumped forward against his seat belt.

Jon reached through the broken window, grabbed the seat belt, and yanked it up into the driver's throat. The man bucked and clutched his throat, clawing at Jon's hands. Jon kept it pressed against his larynx, cutting off his oxygen, and aimed the gun at his friend in the next seat.

Blood poured from the wound in the passenger's forehead and dripped down his nose. The airbag had deflated in his lap. Panting, he looked at Jon with sheer terror in his eyes.

"Where are they?" Jon asked.

"They left," the passenger said in a high-pitched whine.

"Who are you? What are your names?"

"They call me Slim," the passenger said then pointed at the driver. "He's Jerry."

"You said they were here. You said you had them."

"I did, but she pulled a gun. She shot at us!"

"Why aren't you dead?"

"Wha...?" Slim raised his brow then looked over at his struggling friend. Jon still had the seat belt pressed into Jerry's throat. His face turned purple, and his eyes bulged.

"You're killing him!" Slim's pitch rose an octave.

"Yes. I'll stop when you tell me where they are."

"I don't know, man, I don't! Please! I'll do anything!"

Jon released the strap choking Jerry. The driver coughed and gagged until he refilled his lungs with air.

"Do you know where they are?" He pointed the snout of the gun at Jerry's face.

He shook his head.

"Okay, boys. I believe you." He lowered his gun.

Relief crossed their faces, and Slim let out a small whoop. "You do?"

"Yes. But I need something else from you guys."

"Anything. Anything at all," Slim said.

"I need the names of heroin suppliers and addresses. I need everything you got."

"Huh?" Slim asked, puzzled.

Jon lifted his gun and fired a shot into the passenger-side door, and Slim jumped with a shriek.

"No questions." Jon put the gun away and brought something else out. He held up a shiny, sharp object. He grabbed Jerry's left hand and pulled it to him. "I'm going to put a needle underneath each fingernail. I'm going to push it all the way in. Do you understand?"

Jerry quaked in horror, staring at the threading needle. Its metal glimmered in the sunlight.

"I'll put one in each finger for each minute that passes that you don't give me what I ask for." He brought the needle up to Jerry's hand, forced his forefinger out of his closed fist, and prepared to inject.

Slim's face turned a shade of green, and Jerry screamed, "Nooo!"

"Okay, okay! I'll tell you," Slim said between sobs. "I'll tell you everything I know."

Jon smiled and lowered the needle but still held on to Jerry's hand. "I'm impressed. You made a good choice. What are the names of all the suppliers of black in this area, and where can I find them?"

Slim glanced at the ground then scrunched his face. "I don't really know their names. I just see 'em on the streets where I get my high."

"Wrong answer." Jon pulled Jerry's hand closer, brought the needle up, and injected it into the squealing victim. It only took one injection before he received the rest of the information he needed.

CHAPTER FIFTEEN

"Happy Again"
I wish I could make this all go away.
If I could just take away your pain, then maybe you
Would stop using again...
How can I fix this?
How can I make you happy again?
-Poem from Liberty's Diary

Are you okay? The voice in Liberty's head sounded sincere and concerned. She let out a big breath and felt her anxieties leave—just not all of them.

They were back in their motel room. Having the Oldsmobile parked outside felt much better than the van. It had been a big green target. It might as well have been illuminated by a huge spotlight and a red arrow saying, "We're right here!"

Did she want to keep hiding or be found? That was the real question. Her head spun with possibilities. She didn't know which path was the right one to take or where she should go. *What should I do?* Her mother was still on the idea of hiding out and never being found, but Liberty knew being caught was an inevitability.

So, if that's the ultimate end, what are you waiting for? her conscience spoke.

I don't know.

Call the police! End it now while you still can.

My mother would kill me.

This is a dangerous game you're playing, Lib.

I know.

What are you waiting for? the voice echoed.

You asked me that already.

But you didn't answer.

She sighed and rolled her eyes. *Something better. Hope.* She shrugged.

Hope for what?

For my mom.

Do you think she'll get better?

Her shoulders drooped. *No. Not without help.*

Then get help.

From the cops? She felt anger build in her gut. *They'll take her away. They'll put her in jail and me in foster care. That's not good for either of us, and I'll never see her again.*

That's what you're afraid of, isn't it?

Yes.

You love your mom.

Her chest heaved into a sob. Tears streaked her cheeks, and her nose ran. She didn't bother wiping them away at first. She let everything drip into her lap while she sat in the chair next to the window.

Rain pelted the glass, and lightning flashed through the crack of the curtain. The wind blew in gusts, and thunder howled behind it. She peeked through the drapes. Electricity sparked and illuminated the bottoms of clouds like a plane's headlights. Bolts striking, one right after the other, the lightning created a show.

She was reminded of days when she was young, and she and her mother would beam with excitement when thunderstorms hit. At one point, they'd lived in a small house with a front porch that faced east. They would sit next to each other on that porch, eating watermelon and watching the sky light up every few seconds as the thunder bellowed and roared. Lightning stabbed at the ground from all over the valley as if the sky were cracking.

The watermelon was sweet and delicious. They would spit out the seeds on the ground in front of the porch. It was the only time her mom would allow any sort of spitting or littering. When the juice dribbled down their chins, they would wipe the stickiness away. She could see her mom from the past looking at her with a warm smile, her eyes filled with love and her face glowing.

Why is it always watermelon? She didn't know. They'd happened to have a good melon one night when a lightning storm had struck and had chosen to eat it. Since then, lightning storms and watermelons had been attached.

She watched the storm rage outside her motel room. The beautiful thing about Oklahoma was also its worst enemy. The thunder and lightning always brought torrential winds and tornados with them. A tree flailed its branches like a madman wanting to run and escape the storm but was held in place by roots that ran deep.

Are you okay?

Liberty breathed in the scent of the storm and tasted watermelon. *I will be. I think.*

Her phone vibrated. A text came in, and she looked at it. It wasn't the unknown number, but it also wasn't anyone listed in her contacts.

The text read, *Liberty? Are you okay?*

Chills ran up her spine and tickled her scalp. *Is my conscience texting me?* It was too coincidental. Another text vibrated her phone.

This is Detective Clay Baxter.

She put her hand to her mouth. Her heart skipped a beat, then it began to pound like a heavy metal drummer. These were the first words communicated to her by the authorities. There was no doubt in her mind the unknown number had been from a cop, but now he was using a different number and texting.

She refused to open the texts. She quickly read them as they flashed on her screen. She knew that the minute she opened them, it would signal to the sender it had been read, and she didn't want that.

I'm trying to help you. Will you talk to me?

"Stop texting me," she mumbled.

The toilet flushed, and her mother shuffled out of the bathroom. Liberty turned to look at her. She was ghastly white and slick with sweat, and her face was wrenched with nausea. She wiped her mouth with the back of her hand. Sitting across the room, Liberty could see her trembling hands, and her legs wobbled like a newborn calf's.

"Mom? Are you okay?"

"No." She shook her head and plopped onto the bed. "I am really sick."

"What is it? You look like you have the flu. What can I get you?"

"You *know*." She gave Liberty a grave look before her head sank.

Her shoulders started to pump with sobs. She tilted forward, and Liberty cradled her mother's head to her chest.

"I'm not going to make it, Lib. I need it. I've never been this bad before."

"Here. Lie down."

Liberty helped lower her on her back then covered her with the sheet and blanket. JJ clutched the covers in a death grip and held them up to her chin. Her sunken eyes looked up at Liberty.

"I'm so sorry—" Her voice cracked. "So, so sorry. You deserve much better."

"No, Mom. Don't say that." Liberty wanted to tell her she was a great mom—the best mom in the world—but she couldn't.

JJ's body broke into convulsions, and her bangs stuck to her forehead with sweat. "I've been in there throwing up. I have nothing more in my stomach to vomit. I feel like I left two lungs and a liver in there." She let out a small chuckle.

"I need to call an ambulance."

"No!" JJ was adamant. "Do not call anybody! Promise me."

"You need help!" Liberty yelled, tears in her voice.

"I just need a little to get by. Mandy should be calling me any minute. She's a friend. She said she was gettin' some, and she was gonna give me a little."

"Have you called her again?"

"Only ten times. She hasn't answered, the bitch." JJ clenched her eyes shut. "And neither will Jimmy."

"Do you think he stole the money?"

"I don't know. He *was* actin' funny after we left Billy Ray's. If he did, he didn't tell me. Or give me any of it." She shook her head. "He was whining before he left 'bout how broke he was an' couldn't give me more. I hope he goes to hell. Now I'm here, an' I got nothin', and I feel like I'm gonna die."

Liberty felt the money burn a hole in her pocket. "How much does fifty dollars buy?"

JJ's eyes widened, and she looked at Liberty with narrowed eyes. "What do you mean? You got money?"

Liberty paused then spoke in a small voice. "I have some, yes."

"You holding out on me?"

She thought her mother was going to come unhinged, but she held back. "I-I was holding on to it in case we needed it. For food or gas—things. It's the last of our money."

JJ closed her eyes and held her daughter's hand tight. "I'm going to make a call and place an order. When they get here, you'll have to pay them. Can you do that?"

"Yes." She nodded.

Liberty thought how nice it would have been if her mother had said, "No, darling, you're right. You were right to save the money for other things. We're going to need them. I'm sick right now, but I'll get through. I'll be fine." Liberty hated her for not being able to say that.

She walked into the bathroom to fix her mom a cold towel while JJ made the call. Liberty heard the conversation from the other room. She couldn't hear all the words, but at one point, there was hostility. She grabbed a white cloth and turned the cold water on. She waited with a hand under the water until it went ice-cold. Then she put the cloth under it, soaked it, and rung it out thoroughly. She turned the water off then walked to her mom's bedside as JJ hung up.

"Did the call go good?" Liberty asked.

She nodded.

"Here." Liberty folded the cloth and placed it on her forehead.

"Thank you." JJ ran the rag over her face to wipe away the heat and sweat then placed it back on her forehead, hand shaking more than ever. "He won't come to the hotel."

"What? Why?"

"Why?" She gave Liberty a look like she was thinking *you need to ask?* "He's heard we're on the run and are wanted for murder. It was all I could do to convince him to come halfway. There's a donut shop a few blocks down at the corner of Virginia and Murdock. He works that corner. They'll meet you there in the parking lot." She looked at Liberty with defeated, pleading eyes. "I can't make it. I'm too weak, Lib."

"No." Liberty was resolute. "No way! I'm not going to go buy your drugs."

"I wish I could, but you know I can't. There's no other way. I can't even walk."

She knew her mother was right. *Dammit!* She'd promised herself she would never become an enabler, even though deep down she knew she was. She shopped, cooked, and cleaned for her. She paid the bills before the heat and electricity were shut off. *But buy her drugs?* That was *beyond.*

"Can you trust *them*? What if it's a trap like at Slim's?"

"It's not. I promise. He wouldn't risk it. Sal and I go way back. We were close friends for a time. He doesn't usually do this, but he owes me one, and I'm cashin' in on the favor. He'll come through."

"Five hundred bucks is tempting."

"Hey." JJ drilled a look into Liberty. "I promise. You're just gonna have ta' trust me. Slim's a drug head, and Sal is a businessman. Big difference."

"So do I go now?"

"No. He's gonna text me when he's ready. I'll tell you when. Hopefully soon."

Nauseous, Liberty sauntered back to her chair. She felt dizzy. She turned on the TV, and the storm raged outside. The weatherman pointed out spots on his storm tracker with panic spread across his face.

"We have sightings of two tornadoes touching down west of Tulsa near Sand Springs. The storm is heading farther west into Stillwater, and it's only going to get worse. If you are in those areas, you need to find shelter. If you're in your home, stay away from the windows. Go to an inner room or downstairs, if you have one. You need to do this for the next thirty minutes if you live in the area of Sand Springs."

The weatherman continued his storm tracking and warnings, and Liberty shook her head. Tornadoes were on their way. Not only did she have to meet a drug dealer and buy drugs, but she had to do it in the middle of a life-threatening storm. Her belly squirmed, and her intestines tied themselves in knots.

The next hour passed by with excruciating agony. JJ couldn't stay still. She rolled back and forth in bed, shaking and convulsing as if something inside was clawing to get out, and she went into the bathroom and vomited twice. Amidst all that, she moaned and cursed at the drug dealer.

Wind and rain continued to whip back and forth outside. Liberty sat in her chair, wound up like a coil. She surfed the net and Facebook on her phone and watched TV to keep her mind off things, but nothing helped. She turned the TV off, sank into her chair, then closed her eyes. There was silence for several moments.

Honk! Honk! Honk!

Liberty leaped from her seat, searching in panic for the sound. JJ bolted up in bed at the same time. It had come from *inside* the room.

"What the—"

Liberty looked down at her phone on the table. It had come from her phone. Across the screen, it read, *Tornado warning in your area. Take shelter.*

"Shit." She switched the warning off with trembling hands. She turned to JJ, who waited for an answer. "Tornado warning."

Honk! Honk! Honk!

This time, it was JJ's phone.

"Nothing like that to shake your nerves." Liberty sneered at her phone. "Anything from him yet?"

"No. Nothing." JJ groaned.

Then the tornado sirens outside rang. Horns had been placed strategically throughout the city, and they went off like a nuclear missile warning. They started with a low, winding cry, turned into a high-pitched wail, then repeated themselves over and over again. It was an unnerving sound.

Liberty peeked through the drapes again. Debris and leaves blew in a wild array throughout the parking lot. Trees bowed, straightened out, then bowed again like cult followers worshipping their leader. Then hail pelted the ground.

JJ's phone beeped an alert.

"Finally." JJ picked up her phone and looked at it. "It's time. He's there now."

Liberty turned to her mother in horror, and JJ's face reflected the same. Marbles rolled back and forth in Liberty's belly.

"I'm going," JJ said. "You don't have to."

"Yes, I do."

JJ stood up, braced herself on the bed, and hobbled forward. Sweat beaded across her face. She doubled over from a stomach cramp.

"Mom. You won't make it. Not in this storm. You can't drive, let alone walk. I'll go. I can do this. It's not too far."

She helped her mother back to bed and refilled her glass with water. "Drink more of this, okay? I'll be back before you know it."

"Thank you, Lib." Tears fell down JJ's cheeks. "You should never have to do this."

"I know. How much will this cost? What am I getting? Do I have to worry?"

"It's going to cost forty-five dollars, and he's giving you point two grams. Two bags."

"Okay. What's his name?"

"His name is Sal. Don't say his name. You won't have to."

Liberty quickly put her jacket on and approached the door.

"Do you have an umbrella?" her mother asked.

"No. I'll be fine."

"Be careful. I love you."

It was hard to say it at that moment, but Liberty did anyway, "I love you too."

CHAPTER SIXTEEN

Thunder cracked as she exited the motel room, and Liberty jumped. The balcony overhead protected her from the hail, which had turned to sleet. The wind was strong and attempted to knock her down. She looked across the street at the tree she'd seen earlier. It was still for a moment before the wind picked up again. The branches flailed many arms up and down, left and right, and all around. The tree still tried to run from the storm, but its roots held it firmly to the soil. All it could do was stand there and take the beating until the storm uprooted it or split it in half. Liberty could relate.

Their room was on the ground floor, and it was a short walk to their parking spot. Slim's car was as large as a boat. Once inside, she had to extend her legs completely to touch the pedals with the tips of her feet, and she barely peeked over the steering wheel. She was driving down an empty street within a minute. No one else was driving in the storm. She headed down 177 toward Virginia, as instructed.

She saw more trees swaying back and forth, bowing to her as she drove. Leaves and branches blew across the street, and on the left side of the road, a forty-foot pine tree couldn't resist the winds any longer. She watched in terror as it popped out of the ground and crashed onto the center roof of a house.

The car was huge and probably weighed a ton, but amidst the power and ferocity of the storm, it felt like a plastic toy. The right gust of wind could toss her vehicle like a cardboard box.

The rain came down like automatic fire, and she had to keep the wipers on their fastest speed. Thunder boomed again to let her know that she was just a visitor on Earth and not really in control. The elements could take her life at any moment they desired.

Lightning illuminated her surroundings. She looked to the sky and saw a funnel cloud in the distance descending for the ground. If it touched the earth, it would become a tornado, and it wasn't too far from where she was.

Her body clenched. Papers, leaves, branches, boxes, and all kinds of debris tumbled through yards and across the street, and the sirens wailed. She swerved to miss a large fallen branch in the road. The rain and debris blurred her vision, and she leaned forward, pressing her eyes into the darkness to clear the images.

There was the sign for Virginia. She took the exit and headed for Burdock Street, which came up quickly, and she saw the donut shop. It was lit up in yellow with its security lights. The business looked closed for the night, and the building sat in a large parking lot with a single car sitting at its center. The drug dealers picked an open spot, probably to be sure cops didn't tag along or that they didn't attract any unwanted guests.

It didn't calm her fear. It could still be a setup. Maybe cops were inside. *What if... something worse is waiting?*

A blue old-style sports car, maybe from the nineties, held three dark figures inside. Two in the front and one in the back. Her stomach flipped. Her heartbeat raced, and her mouth felt like cotton. Anything could happen. But her mother wouldn't send her there if she didn't feel it was safe. *Would she?*

She's an addict, Lib. She's sick. She'd do anything, even at your expense.

Liberty looked straight ahead. She didn't want her conscience to speak at that moment.

Are you okay?

Shut the hell up!

She drove the car alongside the old sports car and stopped. Her window was parallel to the driver's-side window. Before she could make out his features, she was blinded by a bright light. It illuminated her entire front seat then moved to the back seat. When the beam pulled away, she saw the man in the back seat holding a flashlight. He was huge, muscular, and hunched like a beast. He almost took up the entire back seat. He turned the flashlight off.

The driver was heavyset with a full beard and menacing eyes. She guessed that was Sal. He rolled his window down. She did the same. Rain fell into the car, and the wind howled.

"You JJ's daughter?" he called out loud enough to hear over the wind.

The other two men in the car stared at her. *Do they have guns?* She was vulnerable. They could do anything. Kill her, rape her, or both.

"Y-Yes." She nodded. "Are you Sal?"

Instead of answering, he motioned to her with his thumb rubbing against two fingertips. "Money."

She was tempted to ask to see the drugs first before showing the money. She'd seen too many movies and was in no position to do that. It was unnerving, but she was at their mercy.

"Money!" he called again, irritated at her hesitation.

"Oh! Yes—sorry."

She pulled out the crumpled bills. One twenty, one ten, and three fives. She had to open her car door to reach him, and he snatched the cash away. He rolled up his window, and Liberty thought she'd made a mistake by handing him the cash before getting the drugs. If she didn't get the heroin, her mother could die. The withdrawals were too severe. Liberty would have to give in and call the ambulance, let the cops come and arrest them, and so on.

Sal counted the cash. Apparently satisfied, he rolled his window down then tossed something out. It landed on the ground in the rain.

"Hey!" she called out in reflex then bit her tongue.

The BMW sped away fast with a squeal of tires as Liberty picked up two items from the wet pavement. Two black balls were wrapped up tight in the plastic. That looked right. She quickly closed the door, rolled the window up, and sped out of there. Sal's car was nowhere to be seen. He had disappeared like a ghost, and she was relieved.

She hurried back to the hotel without incident.

AS IF BUYING HEROIN for her mother hadn't been enough, Liberty had to hold the spoon steady for her as she mixed water with the heroin. JJ's hands were too shaky. She placed a lighter underneath the spoon to heat it. It didn't need much. The black rock dissolved quickly, and JJ put the needle of the syringe into the liquid drug to suck it up.

"Thank you," JJ whispered.

Liberty set the spoon down and stepped back. She'd never seen her mother shoot heroin. JJ was always careful to hide it and usually locked herself in the bathroom.

Feeling sick and light-headed, Liberty walked back to her chair and sat down. The sirens outside had stopped, and the wind and rain receded. Liberty turned the TV on to see the weatherman discuss how the tornado warnings were off Stillwater then, but he was going to continue to track the storm. Of course he was.

It must have been too hard for JJ to find a vein in her arms. Instead, she used a vein on the back of her hand just above her knuckles. When she pulled the needle out, she pushed her hand to her mouth and sucked on the tiny, bleeding hole.

Liberty imagined the drug entering JJ's body and spreading its warmth quickly through her highway of veins, stretching to every inch of her body, sedating the convulsions in its path. She saw the anxiety leave JJ's face, and her head seemed to swim with a calming, artificial euphoria. JJ's shoulders sank, and her hands fell to her sides. She had turned from a tight spring to a limp noodle in seconds, and she slid back into bed.

For the time being, Liberty's tension crawled back into its hole. Exhaustion took over. She breathed in heavily and closed her eyes. The rain turned to a soft patter on the window. The palliative sound soothed her to sleep.

CHAPTER SEVENTEEN

Jon sat in his Dodge truck, parked across from Sal's house. He'd been there over an hour and was getting impatient. Sal was the second person on the list he'd received from Slim. He'd already visited the first lead, but it had gone nowhere. He hoped the next would pan out. He was prepared to do anything it took to get the information he needed.

A car pulled into Sal's driveway and parked. The wind had died down significantly, and the rain was light. Jon stepped out. Keeping low, he strode across the lawn to hide behind a large boxwood next to the porch.

Three men exited the car and trotted to the front door. One was a heavyset man fitting Slim's description of Sal. Behind Sal was a large man built like a mountain, and the last guy was half his size. They entered the house, then the smaller man, who was last in line, pushed the door closed.

Seizing the moment, Jon kicked the door back open with tremendous force, and it slammed against the wall. The three jumped and twisted around. Jon flew in and shot a front kick to the smaller man's chest, propelling him off his feet to land on the couch behind him.

The mountain next to Sal was well over six feet tall, an entire head taller than Jon. His tight shirt outlined muscles that could only be achieved through immense training or steroids. He attacked Jon with a right haymaker.

The professional quickly evaded and blocked the blow with his left forearm, then he jabbed his knuckles into the circumflex nerve in his target's armpit. If struck correctly, it would instantly numb the arm. As the man flinched, Jon drove the ball of his foot into his solar plexus, taking all the air out of his lungs, then finished with a punch to the throat.

The big man gasped, clutched his throat, and crumpled to the floor.

Sal backpedaled as Jon withdrew his nine-millimeter Glock with its attached sound suppressor. The smaller man rolled off the couch and stood, but before he could attack or run, the killer fired two rounds, one into each foot. The cartilage, muscle, and bone exploded, and he crumpled to the ground in an instant. He howled and reached for his wounded feet.

Jon pointed the gun at Sal as he marched for the drug dealer.

"What? Who?" Lips quivering and eyes tearing up, Sal held his hands out in surrender. "Don't kill me. Please, please, I'll give you what you want."

Jon didn't say a word. His steel gaze bore into Sal, who continued shuffling backward. The dealer stumbled and fell on the kitchen floor.

Jon kept his weapon trained on him. "Get up. Sit down over there." He motioned to the small dining table.

Sal did as instructed. "You want drugs? Money? What?" His words tumbled out, and he kept his eyes on the ground. He wouldn't look at the pistol aimed at him.

The small man continued to cry in the front room. Jon exhaled noisily at the distracting sound. It was shrill, and he was convinced that no sensible conversation could be had with that racket. Jon took two steps back, glanced into the front room, and aimed his gun. He fired two shots that ended the wailing. He turned back to Sal.

"Shit, man! Why did you have to do that?"

"You're still alive. For the moment. I just need some information. Simple." He shrugged and looked around the kitchen. While keeping the gun and an eye on Sal, he opened drawers and cabinets but found nothing satisfying.

He approached Sal again. Jon glared at him with his one good eye.

Sal gawked at Jon's dead, frozen blue eye. "What are you looking for?"

"For something I can use to get information out of you. In cases like this, I have always found that no one, even in the best of situations, is compliant at first. Everyone needs a little nudge."

"I don't even know what you want! Try me."

"Mmmm." He thought about it. "I'm not sure. Because you see, if I ask you, and you don't tell me what I want to hear, it's going to really piss me off. That's when things get real messy. And I hate messy. So I thought, if I start with a little torture, I could end your suffering a lot quicker. I'll be in and out of here in no time. How nice would that be?"

"Look, mister, I'll tell you anything. Really."

Jon looked around the room again. "I just can't find anything in this kitchen. You don't have a meat grinder, do you?"

"*Grinder?*" The blood drained from Sal's face.

"You've heard of me?"

"Y-Yes. Please don't kill me." Tears welled up and ran down his cheeks.

"Trust me. You *want* me to kill you. It's the alternative you don't want to live through."

Hearing footsteps behind him, Jon moved in a blink and stepped out of the way as a bat came down. The large man had recovered and attacked. The bat clattered against the tile floor, and the big man lurched forward. Jon cracked the big man's kneecap with a left kick, yanked the bat from his grasp, then swung it up against his chin with a *crack*. The large man toppled like a tree, blood flying in the air.

Jon kept cool and collected. He didn't breathe hard, didn't sweat, and didn't panic. He approached Sal, slapping the bat up and down in his open palm. "Guess what. I found something." He smiled.

Sal's face turned a shade of green.

"Place your right hand out on the table, palm down, and spread your fingers. Right there." He motioned.

"Please. I'll tell you anything. Just ask. I *beg* you."

"Okay, you're right. Maybe you'll be the first to tell me what I need right off the bat. No pun intended. It would be so refreshing. So here's the deal. Put your hand out like I said. I'll ask you the question, and if you answer correctly, I won't bring the bat down. Fair enough?"

He nodded and put his hand out flat against the table.

"Extend your arm all the way."

Sal did.

"Now, hold still. If my bat comes down, you better not move your hand. Are you going to move your hand?"

"No. No, I wouldn't do that."

"Everybody says that. But instinct takes over, and they move their hand. Trust me. You don't want what comes next if you move your hand. So please, for your own sake, don't do it."

"I won't. I won't. I promise."

"Okay. You ready?"

"Yes." Sal nodded nervously.

Jon shoved the gun into the back of his pants so he could hold the bat in both hands.

"Here comes the million-dollar question. Where is Jemma Justice and her daughter?"

Sal scrunched his face. "Who?"

Jon let out a deep sigh then quickly brought the bat up to swing.

"No, no, no, wait!" Sal shrieked. "JJ you mean? She's at a motel!"

The bat came down.

CHAPTER EIGHTEEN

The house was quiet and empty except for Detective Clay Baxter, who plopped a handful of ice in his glass and filled it up with water at the kitchen sink. He listened to the rain pattering against his windows and stared outside for a long time. He finally stepped out of the kitchen and walked over to the sofa in his living room. The soft light of one lamp was the only illumination. The darkness in the rest of his house accompanied the silence.

A picture of him and his late wife, Samantha, smiled at him from the end table. It had been two years since her passing. A tragic hiking accident had taken her life suddenly, leaving him no moment for a last goodbye, a final kiss, or one more I love you. Despite everyone's advice and his own rational thought, he felt guilt, and it bled like an ulcer.

He looked at her picture every night, told her he loved her, and blew her a kiss. Time was healing him but only so much. Her passing left a physical pain in his heart that never went away.

He picked his smartphone up from the coffee table and looked at his text messages. No answer from Liberty, and no sign she had read it. He *knew* she had, though. He felt it. *How could she not?* An overwhelming voice inside urged him not to give up. He had to keep trying. Liberty was the key. JJ hadn't answered any calls or texts, either, and he'd submitted for a warrant to track her phone. But if he could communicate with Liberty, he felt he could talk her in. But he had to communicate something intelligent to elicit a response.

He didn't know what to say or how to start. He searched for the magic words to touch and inspire her to write back. He started, erased, and started again several times until he felt like he had something good.

I know what you're going through. I've been there myself. I want to help.

It was the truth, and it was from the heart.

LIBERTY'S EYES FLUTTERED open at her vibrating phone. She sat up and looked around. Her mom was asleep on the bed. The phone alerted her a second time of the text, and she lifted it up. It was the cop again.

I know what you're going through. I've been there myself. I want to help.

Liberty scowled at her phone and slammed it down. *Really?* she thought with a biting, facetious attitude. *You killed a drug dealer when you were thirteen while he was roughing up your heroin-addicted mother?*

Her phone buzzed again. The officer wasn't giving up. *My mother was addicted to prescription meds at first. It turned into heroin later. I saw things as a kid that no child should ever have to witness.*

"Hmmm," she said. She wasn't sure what to make of it. Maybe he was playing with her to get her to talk. The cops had professional negotiators that did this sort of thing. They used them to talk down nutcases from jumping off a ledge and to negotiate hostage situations.

She was a prostitute, the detective continued. *That's how she made enough money to pay for her habit. Men came in and out of our house all the time. I was physically abused repeatedly by men and by her.*

Geeze, she thought. *That's horrible.*

His next text piqued her interest even more. *I'm not saying that's your life or your mother is anything like mine. I only say that because I know what it's like to be a child of an addict.*

She was dying to find out what had happened to his mother—what had happened to *him.* She wanted to text back and ask, but she was afraid. *What would it hurt?* It wasn't like he could trace her. She just needed to be strong and not let him in her head and talk her down.

She stared at the phone for a long time, waiting for more of the story to be sent. It never came. Perhaps he was done. But he hadn't asked her to answer back. *Why?* She knew it was his job to get her to talk. Maybe it was still a psychological game of chess, and to win, he had pulled back to wait. She shook her head. *Lib, you are thinking way too hard about this. Just freaking text him back.*

She swiped on the text, opening the conversation, knowing it signaled to the cop that his text had been read. She'd crossed the point of no return.

So what happened to your mom? she texted.

He responded right away. *She died when I was eleven. Drug overdose.*

The words stabbed her heart, and she swallowed hard. That *could* happen to her mom. JJ had come close before. It was always in the back of Liberty's head. The fear sat parked behind her thoughts, waiting for the right moment to pounce.

I'm sorry, Liberty texted.

Thank you.

So, what happened to you? She was afraid to ask, guessing she knew the answer. It took a couple of minutes before the response came.

Foster care. I moved around a lot to different families. One time, I stayed with an older couple who were sweet and loving. I stole from them and ran away. They went after me. Searched all night and finally caught me at the bus station. I thought, this is it. They're going to throw me back into the system, and I'll shuffle on to the next family. But they didn't. They stood by me as I struggled. They put me into therapy, grounded me when I was bad, rewarded me when I was good, brought me back two more times from running away, saved my life several times when I tried to end it, and yet still they stayed. Still kept me in their home. Fed me, loved me, cared for me. This kind of life was so new to me, and I was afraid of it. Afraid of losing it, I guess. Guilty for losing my mom. Sad she didn't have that life too.

Liberty was awestruck. She didn't know what to say, but she *felt* this man was telling the truth, and it resonated with her. The story was too harsh and too personal to be fictionalized to gain common ground.

Did you end up staying with that family? she asked.

Yes. I eventually called them my parents. I still do.

Do you hate your mom?

There was another long wait for the answer.

I had a lot of hate and anger for the longest time. Oddly enough, I think it was directed at me. I hated what she did. Hated what she became and hated myself for still loving her. That's the strange part. I couldn't help but love her. She was my mom. So I felt guilty for feeling love and guilty for feeling hate. It took a long time to separate the two and love her for who she was while only hating her actions and decisions. She was sick. Addiction is a disease, and even with years of therapy, I still have a hard time coming to terms. But I keep going. I keep living.

Liberty paused. She didn't know what to say. Her mind was busy processing it all and what it meant for her—what it could mean for her relationship with her mom. Their situation was completely different than the cop's.

Liberty? Are you and your mother okay?

She waited to answer. Then, *Yes. We're fine.*

I only want to help. I hope you understand.

Resentment filled her again as she typed her response. *Help? You just want to bring me and my mother in.*

Her phone buzzed immediately. *No. I want to bring you both in because I want you safe. I care about what happens to you.*

You don't even know me, she texted.

True. I don't know you, but I want to try. My name is Clay Baxter. When I first started on your case, I saw myself in you. I know the hell you're going through. I was lost, too, at one time, and someone helped me. I want to pay that forward and help someone else, and that's you.

Liberty fired back a message. *Look, you had a nightmare childhood. I get that, and I'm sorry. You want to try to make up for that by jumping into my life with your superman cape and save the day? Well I'm not your prize!*

Angry thoughts spun in Liberty's head and she set the phone down. She had been drawn into the cop's personal story, but maybe he'd just told it as a ploy to bring her in after all. She wanted to trust him but wasn't sure she could. The phone vibrated, and she waited for a minute before picking it up. It was the cop again.

Liberty, I know you didn't do it. You didn't kill that man. And neither did your mother. I have the medical examiner's report. He states in his findings that it was an accident. I just want to bring you two in safely.

Liberty bit her lip while pondering this latest bit of information.

Is this true? Liberty texted.

A long pause then, *Yes.*

We want a lawyer.

You'll have one. The state will assign someone if you don't already have a lawyer.

Liberty typed the next message slowly then hit send. *What will happen to my mom?*

After a minute, his response came back. *Detox first. Then, we'll get her help to stay clean. We'll figure that out along the way. We just need to get you two safe.*

What happens to me? Foster care? Liberty asked.

No one said they're taking away your mother.

I'm not stupid.

Another minute passed, then Clay's next message appeared. *Of course not. It is clear you are not. As for what happens to you or your mother, none of us can make those judgments at this point. There's a lot to sort out. You must trust me. Have faith. I'm not going to let either of you slip through the cracks. I'm going to get help for your mother and help for you. I want to give you what I never had. I will never give up on you, Liberty.*

Tears filled Liberty's eyes. There was hope in that statement. She was afraid to rely on it, but the promise of it was too good. She *wanted* to believe it.

There is something else I need to tell you, Clay texted. *It was something I was afraid might happen. It's just been brought to my attention. You and your mother's lives are in immediate danger.*

What do you mean? Liberty asked.

After a long pause, his response came. *Billy Ray Pines. His family believes you and your mother are responsible for his death. They hired a professional killer to find you.*

Liberty's heart stopped, and she gasped. If it was a hoax to bring them in immediately, it was a cruel one. If it was *true*, it was a real terror.

She thought of the reward promised to Slim and Jerry to divulge their whereabouts. *It must have been from the killer, not the cops. This was* real.

Her phone vibrated. *Liberty, this is no joke. I need to bring you and your mother in now. Where are you?*

Liberty didn't answer him.

He has already killed three men. Drug dealers. He is on his way. Where are you?

Her face flushed. She thought of the three men she'd bought drugs from earlier. *Were Sal and his two cohorts the three dead bodies?* They had to be. Her thoughts raced, but she still couldn't trust him.

She typed out another message. *What if you're not who you say you are? What if you're the killer?*

There was a pause, then finally, a text returned with an image. Liberty opened the image to reveal a picture of Detective Clay Baxter's badge. It looked official. He was telling the truth.

She held her fingertips over the keyboard on her phone and hesitated. She was about to type out their motel address.

"What are you doinnng?" JJ's voice slurred.

Liberty jumped in surprise and turned to see her mother standing behind her with an accusing look. JJ looked over Liberty's shoulder, and her eyes fixed on the image of the badge. She exploded in rage and grabbed the phone.

DURING HIS TEXT CONVERSATION with Liberty, Clay had received a call from Jim Calloway informing him of three drug dealers who'd been shot and killed near Sunset Park. Jim had said it looked like a professional hit, and that comment struck Clay. Hank had told him that Rick would want revenge, and he would hire a ruthless professional to do it. The dealers could be a way the killer was tracking them. Clay had chosen to share that information with Liberty in hopes it would scare her enough to turn herself and her mother in.

Calloway texted him the address of the crime scene. He threw his jacket on and raced to his car while dialing Liberty's number. He had no more time to waste texting. He hoped he'd gotten through to her enough that she would pick up the phone so they could talk. But Liberty didn't answer.

He redialed several times as he drove but continued to come up empty.

"Please Liberty, I need you to answer the phone! Where are you?"

Her phone didn't ring anymore. It went straight to her voice mail.

CHAPTER NINETEEN

JJ snatched the phone from Liberty after seeing the image of the badge. Liberty's first emotion was fright at being caught, but it quickly turned to fury. *How dare she do this to me?*

"You've been talkin' to cops?" JJ asked.

"Yes, but it's not what you think."

"It's exactly what I think. You're fixin' to turn us over to the cops. You know what they're gonna do, don't ya?"

"No, I don't, Mom. Enlighten me." Liberty crossed her arms.

"They're not gonna arrest me—they're after you!" JJ stabbed a finger at Liberty's chest. "You killed that man. I wasn't anywhere near him when it happened!"

Liberty felt like a boulder had flown out of nowhere, smashing her chest and knocking her back a few feet. She jabbed her forefinger at JJ. "How can you say that? You were right there!"

"I was on the ground, and you threw a pan at him. It made him fall!"

"*Mom?*"

"I should just call the cops right now," JJ said. "I'll turn *you* in. How 'bout that?"

Liberty started to cry. The pain of the words shook her soul. Her chest sank, and she couldn't catch her breath.

"I've been protectin' you this whole time. Keepin' the cops from gettin' *you*." JJ shrugged. "So if you wanna call and turn yourself in, go right ahead."

"Okay!" Wiping tears from her eyes, Liberty composed herself. "Give me back my phone. I'm turning myself in because I can't keep doin' this!"

"Doin' what?"

"Running! Hiding! Buying you drugs!"

"Oh, that's what it's really all about isn't it? Here we go." JJ threw her hands up. "Let's hear it. Druggy mother, right here. I got all the problems, and I'm the cause of everthin'."

"No, you're not the cause of everything! But a lot of it. You have a drug problem."

"Oh, I do, do I? I've been nothin' but a good mom to you, and this is how you treat me?"

"A 'good mom'? Is that what you call it? Were you a good mom on my eleventh birthday? Remember that? When I had all my friends over for a sleepover?"

"Friends." JJ guffawed. "All three of 'em."

"Wow." She shook her head in unbelievable dismay. "They were my good friends, and we were going to watch movies, play games, pop popcorn, and the whole thing."

"I popped your popcorn!"

"No, you nearly burnt the house down because you couldn't figure the machine out. You spilled the entire bag of kernels all over the kitchen floor. We came in to help clean it up, and you were leaning on the counter with your eyes half-closed, about to fall asleep!"

"Oh please." JJ denied it as she always did.

"We woke you up, and you flung your arm out and knocked over the popcorn popper. Shelly bent down to pick it up, and you tripped and fell on top of her. It was all over after that. They packed up their stuff and left. The worst part was—" She paused, remembering. "The looks on their faces. They *knew*. Even then, they knew."

"Bullshit! They left 'cause Shelly's a stuck-up little bitch. Sorry to say it, but it's true. You ever meet her mom?"

"Who even are you?" Liberty scrunched her face in astonishment.

"Oooh, my poor Liberty." JJ heightened her voice in a condescending tone. "Did Mommy embarrass your friends because I spilled some damn popcorn? Poor little Liberty. 'You need to get help, Mommy,'" she mimicked. "'You need to go to rehab and get all better, and then we can all live happily ever after!' Right? Everything will be all rosy then!"

"*Bitch*," Liberty blurted, eyes burning and wet.

JJ's hand came out of nowhere in a blur, and the open palm smacked Liberty's left cheek so hard the sound echoed in the room. Liberty stumbled as her head snapped to the right from the force of the blow, and her cheekbone stung. Shocked, she didn't know whether to cry or scream, but soon, anger bubbled from the depths of her stomach, and rage overtook her body.

"Happy now?" Liberty asked. "You can deal with this on your own. I am out of here. From now on, you can do your own shopping, pay the bills, clean the house, cook the food, screw your boyfriends, and get kicked out for not paying rent *again*. Buy your own drugs. Shoot your body full of poison till you die. I don't care!" she screamed in a mix of emotions and tears. "Go to hell! I am done!"

"*Good!* Go." JJ gestured with a forward shuffle of her hands. "Get out of here. See how far you get without me. I still put a roof over your head and food on the table."

"Wow, you keep me alive! Mother of the year, right here!" Her sarcastic tone was cutting. "That's all I have of you anymore. I don't have a mom!" Her lips trembled.

JJ said nothing. Her face was a portrait of red rage. She kept her arms folded and held her glare.

"I'm done with it, Mom. I am sick of it. Aren't *you*?" Liberty pointed at her.

JJ threw her hands up again. "I'm sick of this conversation, I'll tell ya that. Sick of hearing what a bad mom I am all the time. After all I've done for you. I can't believe my own daughter is stabbing me in the back. Wants to turn me in. Maybe the cops will arrest me for being a bad mom. 'You're under arrest, Miss Justice, for being a bad mommy. For not showin' enough love and affection, for not providin' her with the latest fashionable clothes or hip electronic devices, and you've never taken your daughter to Disneyland!'" She laughed bitterly. "I didn't realize those were crimes!"

"Mom." Anger seared in Liberty's body again. "What *is* against the law is having heroin in the house and doing drugs around your daughter. And don't forget about the homicide attempt from your psycho drug dealer!" Liberty wanted to point out that *she* had been the one who had gotten them out of the house before the cops showed up and found them a motel to hide in, but it would escalate the situation.

There was a break in the argument. Silence screamed in the room. Liberty's heart was beating out of her chest, and adrenaline electrified her veins. JJ crossed her arms and pursed her lips. The spinning thoughts in Liberty's head slowed down and started to settle in their usual places, and she remembered what Clay had told her about a killer tracking them down. Three dead drug dealers had been found, and she was pretty sure they'd known which motel she and her mom were staying at. Fear pulsed through her all at once and pushed out the rest of her thoughts.

"Mom, we gotta go," she said softly.

JJ glared daggers at her and said nothing.

"The cop told me our lives are in danger. There's a killer after us."

"Really? The *cop* told you?"

"Those three guys I bought the drugs from, they were just found dead."

JJ fell silent.

"He said Billy Ray's family hired a professional to kill us for revenge."

"The cop could be lyin'. Did ya ever think a' that?"

"Yes, but I don't think he is. Did those guys know what motel we are at?"

Her mom said nothing. She stared at the floor for a moment and then, "Shit. I think I did tell them. But that still doesn't mean—"

"Mom. We have to go. We're out of money, and we have to leave in the morning anyway. We're only paid up through tonight."

"True." JJ nodded. "Plus, you've been talkin' to the cops, so they already know where we're at, and they'll be here any minute."

Liberty sighed and rolled her eyes.

"Let's pack up and get the hell outta here. We'll continue this conversation later," JJ said, wiping sweat from her forehead.

CHAPTER TWENTY

The middle-aged man who worked the desk at Sleep Inn slid down to the floor, still convulsing with the little life left in him. Blood ran from the hole in his head, and the wall behind him was covered with it.

"Thank you," Jon said calmly.

The desk manager had been compliant. It hadn't taken much coaxing to get the information he'd required. As a matter of fact, it might have been the easiest interrogation of his career. It was probably because the man had been innocent. He didn't live in the same underworld as Jon's usual victims.

The security camera system was in the next room adjacent to the lobby. It was set up through a computer, which was easy enough to control. Several bullets blew the entire thing into enough pieces that Jon was sure he'd destroyed any visual evidence.

Jon stepped outside and strolled through the rain toward the north end of the motel. It was silent except for the patter of raindrops and the gush of excess water from the gutters. He cut the air with his steel gaze, scanning from left to right for any witnesses, distractions, or hazards that could foil his plan.

He counted the rooms. He was at room eight, and they were at the far end in room twenty-two. There were only four vehicles in the parking lot. There was a blue Toyota Corolla in front of room twelve then a three-quarter-ton Chevy Silverado parked down by room nineteen. The truck was jacked up high off the ground with giant tires, and he could only make out the low front bumpers of the other two cars beyond it.

He knew they'd switched vehicles. They'd left Slim and his stoner friend the van and had taken his car. It hadn't taken more than the first needle to pull all the information he'd needed from them, including a description of his vehicle, but he hadn't seen an Oldsmobile in the lot when he'd driven in.

His thoughts wandered to JJ and Liberty. He had been surprised to see their names on the hit list. He had longed for the right moment for revenge for so many years that he'd given up hope. Karma had finally rewarded him. After his time with JJ, he'd focused on building his new career, and it was thriving. Beyond the great money, it fed him a high beyond what drugs or alcohol could ever reach. To be in control of his own fate was one thing, but to control the fates of others was *godlike*. The world was his puppet, and he held the strings.

Fate had stepped on his neck his entire life until he'd grabbed hold of its throat and twisted. He'd put it under his own foot and, in turn, had gained Fate's respect. *This* was his reward.

He approached room twenty-two. The large window had its drapes pulled shut, and light escaped the edges. It was a good sign they were inside, but it also meant someone was awake. It didn't bother Jon either way. They were not going to be as fortunate as before in surviving his vengeance. He would be quick and get them by surprise.

He slid the master key card into the device on the door quickly, without a sound, and the light turned green. What happened next was one fluid motion. He pushed the handle down, kicked the door, dropped into a crouch, and aimed his pistol.

He swept the room left to right. No one. The room was empty. No luggage, no clothes, no sign that anyone was still in the room. The bathroom was dark and was the last spot unchecked. He jumped into the tiny space, ready to fire, but no one was there.

He flipped the light on and looked at the mirror. It had a message scribbled in lipstick.

Fuck You.

A smiley face was drawn below it.

CHAPTER TWENTY-ONE

They'd left the motel quickly. Driving through the night, they didn't run into anyone on the road. Liberty glanced behind them and saw no one following. Still, JJ sped recklessly. The Oldsmobile was a beast. Its front end stuck out like a second car, and every bump in the road caused the entire vehicle to bounce. JJ and Liberty stared ahead in silence. Liberty's left cheek burned from the hard slap she'd received from her mother back at the motel. The tension in the car was palpable, and neither one would break it or even look at the other.

Liberty kept her gaze out the side window. Houses and buildings flew by in a blur. Though the darkness of the night surrounded them and the traffic was sparse, JJ checked her rearview mirrors frequently. The only sound to keep them company was the clicking of the turn signal, an occasional squeal of the tires on a sharp turn, and the irregular rumbling of the car's engine that probably hadn't gotten a tune-up in years.

Liberty glanced at her mom, and JJ returned the look, her eyes softening. "I'm... I'm sorry for hitting you."

Liberty looked down and said nothing.

"I said some pretty ugly things back there. Sorry for that too."

Liberty turned to stare out the window.

"You know I still need ya, don'tcha?" JJ's lips trembled, as if she was on the verge of crying.

Nearly a minute passed before Liberty nodded and said, "I still need you too. Sorry for what I said. I was just angry." She cringed and added, "I guess I'm just scared."

"Me too." JJ released air and the rest of the tension with it. "I love you."

"Love you more." Liberty grinned.

"Love you most."

"Still love you more."

"To the moon and back." JJ's smile widened.

CHAPTER TWENTY-TWO

C lay stood outside of Salvatore "Sal" Camargo's house while the police and the CSI team buzzed in and out of the home. Two men pushed a bagged body on a gurney from the front door to the ambulance. Red and blue lights from the squad cars cut the darkness, and the rain slowed to a soft rhythm.

Across the street, Calloway was interviewing an older, heavyset lady in a sweat outfit and her tiny husband behind her. They stood just inside their doorway while Calloway was stuck holding their screen door open as the rain fell on him. Clay could hear bits of the conversation. The lady was loud and animated.

"I came out here 'cause of some yellin' then the most awful screamin' I've ever heard. That's when I called you all. Then a minute later, a man came out, jumped in a black truck, and drove off."

"Could you make out what type of truck it was?" Calloway asked.

"Dodge pickup. Four-door," the husband spoke up.

Clay looked at his phone and dialed Liberty. It went straight to voice mail again. He sent another text to her. *Please just let me know you're okay. Give me any hint as to where you're at, and I'll find you.*

He looked into the black night and wondered where she was. He pictured the killer shooting JJ and Liberty as he'd done with Sal's gang. He tried to push those thoughts away. He wondered why she wasn't answering and imagined the killer picking up Liberty's phone and turning it off. Maybe he'd broken it or thrown it into the trees. *Is he torturing them?* He wouldn't allow himself to think of it. He could have tied them up and taken them somewhere. If he had, at least then she was still alive. Somehow, somewhere she was alive, and he stood a chance to save them.

Clay climbed into his car to get out of the rain. He'd interviewed Rick Pines earlier in the investigation and saved his phone number. Clay looked it up and called him. Rick answered on the third ring.

"Hello?"

"Mr. Pines?"

"Who's this?"

"This is Detective Clay Baxter. I'm investigating your brother's death."

"You found the ladies that killed him?"

"Mr. Pines, right now they are persons of interest. And no, we haven't found them. Instead, we're picking up pieces left behind by a professional assassin. Three dead bodies in fact."

"I don't know how that has anything to do with my brother's *murderer*."

"Cut the bullshit. We both know you hired a professional to murder a mother and her thirteen-year-old daughter."

"*Excuse me!* You're supposed to be finding my brother's killers, remember? You told me you were gonna bring them to justice, but it sounds like you're busy pointin' fingers at me!"

"I've made it very clear that I haven't ruled anyone out. And that includes you."

"How hard can it be?" Rick continued to rant. "If you can't find a doped-up mother and her little girl, I'll hire my own investigator."

Clay didn't play into Rick's hand. He pressed forward with what he wanted to say. "Call off your dog, and end this right now. No one would be the wiser, and I'll bring in the woman and child. But if you go through with this and have them killed, it will all lead back to you, and I promise I'll nail you to the wall for it. So I'm giving you a chance. Call him off, and you may walk away clean. So, what will it be, Mr. Pines?"

"Don't threaten—"

"Call it off."

Rick's voice rose with anger. "I don't have any—"

"Call it off."

"Listen. I—"

"Last chance."

There was silence. Clay waited.

"There is nothing to call off," Rick said at last.

"Call it off," Clay repeated and ended the call.

CHAPTER TWENTY-THREE

Jon searched the motel room thoroughly. They'd left some trash, but that was about it. He found two used needles wrapped in tissues in the bathroom garbage bin, so he knew he was on the right track. *Think*, he told himself. He knew he'd barely missed them. The wet prints of their shoes on the carpet told him it had to have been within the last half an hour. Either it was his dumb luck, or someone had tipped them off. *Who and how?*

If he'd only waited to destroy the video surveillance, he could have viewed it to see which direction they'd gone. He cursed at himself and threw a lamp across the room, smashing it against the wall.

Get ahold of yourself, Jon. That's not going to do you any good. He fingered his gun, soothing himself, and dreamt of the moment he would kill JJ. *It'll happen.* He knew Jemma Justice. After all, he'd lived with her for four years, even though more than two of those years he'd spent deployed in the Iraq war. *Where would she go?*

He crossed the room to the table where an array of brochures were spread out like the kind one would find in a lobby. Several of them were for local attractions, but one caught his eye. It was a brochure for Boomer Lake Park, a local recreational park within the city limits. There was a picture of the lake on the front and several people boating and fishing.

Then it hit him. Boomer Lake reminded him of the picture at Jemma's house of her and Liberty with trees in the background and a little piece of the lake on the left side. He was familiar with the recreational spot in the photo. He'd taken them there several times. It was Lake Mc-

Murtry Park. It was Jemma's favorite place to go. A place to camp, fish, and drink into the wee hours of the night.

He knew the police would show up to the motel room, and he had an idea. It might not work. *It's flimsy at best, but what the hell?*

There was a pen on the nightstand, and he circled Boomer Lake Park on the brochure, rumpled it up, and shoved it into the drawer of the nightstand. He knew the police would search this room, as he had. If he got lucky, the police would see the brochure as a clue and head in the wrong direction.

He exited the room carefully. He glanced at the lobby and saw a young couple walk through the front doors. They were about to discover the dead night manager.

"Shit." He looked up at the sign for the motel and the flashing red words that read Vacancy. *Why didn't I turn that off? Am I losing my knack?*

He paused for a moment to contemplate. He could kill them. He had the advantage and still had the silencer attached to his gun. Plenty of ammo too. He didn't have to reload. They were young, early twenties. The man was sharp, clean-cut, and wearing a polo shirt and jeans. She was pretty, in a blue blouse and leggings. Neither of them fit the profile of someone who carried a gun or would put up much of a fight.

He pictured himself stepping in through the lobby door and popping two bullets into the chest and one into the head of each victim. Five seconds at most. He would take their bodies and stuff them behind the counter with the night manager. It would buy him some time before the police were called, but it could also put him at further risk if someone showed up while he was disposing of the bodies.

He wasn't worried about the police at that point, and the risk was not worth taking. Fate would take care of him like it always had. *Move on.*

He stepped into his truck and started the engine. He saw the face of the young woman in the lobby window as he backed out and drove away. Her gaze was fixed on the floor, and her mouth and eyes were open wide in shock and terror. She'd seen the dead night manager, and there was a possibility she would turn and see him too. There was a second moment of hesitation. *Kill or not kill?* He chose not to.

"Fate, don't lead me wrong," he mumbled.

CHAPTER TWENTY-FOUR

Clay felt as if the night would never end. The call came in while he was collecting evidence of the crime scene at Sal's house. There'd been another murder. That time, it was at the Sleep Inn not far from there. His heart stopped, stabbed by the fear it might be Liberty and JJ.

Why do I care about Liberty and her mom so much? Clay had never met them. Never known them before. It was quite possible that Liberty and JJ were both addicts and carried a string of crimes behind them. Perhaps they'd purposefully and knowingly killed Billy Ray Pines over drugs and money. He'd seen that plenty in his career, so it wouldn't be a surprise.

But there was something different about this case. It had started with a feeling when he'd first seen pictures of Liberty and her mom in the house and when he'd read Liberty's poetry. He saw himself in her. In her most recent pictures, she appeared self-possessed, bright, and lovely. Her schoolteacher and principal had been interviewed, and they'd had nothing but good things to say about her besides a recent fight she'd been in. Liberty was something special, and she was an innocent in this lake of sludge and filth her mother had created. She was a victim, as Clay himself had been.

Visions of different men stepping into their apartment when he was six years old resurfaced. His mother had taken the men's hands and led each to the back room. He heard the sounds, and some of them were so harsh and loud that he feared they were hurting his mom. Her bedroom was always locked, but Clay would stand outside of it and pound on the door. His mom would yell back that she was fine and tell him to go back to playing.

One night, a recurring customer came in. Clay had seen him several times before. The man was bald, middle-aged, and large—over six feet tall and close to three hundred pounds. He always reeked of alcohol. Clay could smell it even now. The guy's heavy feet staggered across the living room to Clay, a smile creeping up his cheeks and a gleam of drunkenness sparkling in his eyes. That piece of work would always ruffle Clay's hair with his hand and say "hey, champ" as if to get his approval for what he was going to do to Clay's mom.

The guy knew Clay's mom was a drug addict. Every man who entered their house did, and they knew she was desperate. She would do anything for the money to get her drugs.

Clay glared at the bald man then refocused on the toys he'd been playing with. He said nothing as his mother came out and led the customer to her room. A few minutes later, shrieking and immense thumps escaped his mom's room. The door was unlocked that time. He opened it and froze at what he saw. Growing up, he pushed that image further down in the basement of his mind. He tried to keep it from bubbling to the surface, but he wasn't always successful. No child should ever see their parent in that private act.

At six years of age, he didn't understand what was going on, but he knew wrong from right. He knew bad feelings from good ones well, and this was not of the latter. His mother was tied up to the bed, and the bald man was acting violently. In the quick glimpse, it appeared he was *hurting* her. Clay screamed, and it stopped all motion.

Then, his mother yelled his name at the top of her lungs. "*Clay!* Get on *outta* here! You know better!"

Clay retreated to the living room, hyperventilating. But the large man was not satisfied. He bolted out of that room and charged Clay. He could still see the rage in his eyes and his massive arm, like the trunk of a tree, swinging for his head. Mother was tied up to the bed, helpless, but she wouldn't have done anything anyway.

The man beat Clay with a few more blows and hollered, "You gonna stay quiet now, boy! *Huh?* Stay outta your momma's room now, ya hear?"

Still drunk, the man had shaken his head then stumbled back to the bedroom.

The nightmares were always there, grinning at Clay with a menacing smile. He'd faced them, and it'd taken time, but he'd learned not to let them control him.

That was why he fought for Liberty. She had to know there was a better world, one without monsters. It had taken a long time for Clay to find that out. He'd lived in a bubble for an eternity with eyes that only saw pain, anguish, and fear, never trusting anyone. There was a world beyond, and if he could help someone else find it, perhaps he could shake off his own nightmares a little better.

When Clay arrived at the motel, he and Calloway approached the young couple who'd called in after finding the body. The woman sat on the hood of her car. She shook uncontrollably, and her husband placed an arm around her shoulders.

Clay asked Calloway to question the couple. Clay didn't have the patience. He quickly inspected the lobby and the crumpled body of the night manager behind the counter.

A tall, slender man with dark hair and a mustache entered the lobby with eyes wide and his mouth hanging open.

Clay turned to him before he could see the body. "You're the owner?"

"Yes," the man said. "I'm Daryl Moss. I got your call."

"My partner, Detective Calloway, called you. There's been an incident."

Daryl's shocked eyes drifted to the blood splatter on the wall. He put his hand to his mouth, and his shoulders sank.

"One of your employees has been shot. Let's step outside." Clay motioned and led Daryl out into the parking lot. "There's no need for you to see that. Let my men identify him. Right now, I need some help from you. I need to find out which rooms are occupied and by whom. We need to lock down your motel for the time being while we pursue the investigation. No one comes in or out, is that understood?"

"Yes." Daryl nodded. "I-I'll need to get in there. To access the computer."

"Of course. Give me one second." Clay turned to an officer and called him over. "I need a sheet. Cover the body, please."

Clay entered the lobby and arranged the monitor so it faced the front of the desk. He strung the mouse and keyboard up to the counter for the owner to use without having to step around the dead body.

In a matter of minutes, Clay and three police officers cleared the entire motel. There were only ten occupied units, and on the third try, they found Liberty and JJ's room. The owner said it was booked under the name of "Penny Barnes." It was no surprise that the fugitives had used a fake name.

Fear and anxiety raced through his system before they busted in the door. He expected to see two more dead bodies. Finding Liberty and Jemma like that was going to crush him. He'd been so close. He could have saved them. *If only...*

The room was as empty. Temporary relief washed over him.

They began a search for clues. A few minutes later, Calloway approached him with a rumpled brochure in his hand. "This might be somethin'."

Clay took the brochure and read it. "Boomer Lake Park?"

"Yeah, you think they went there?"

"It's possible. Kind of stupid of them to circle this and leave it behind. Seems suspicious to me."

"It's worth a shot to send a couple of patrols over there to sweep the place," Calloway said.

"For right now, it's the only lead we have. Just send two cars. I doubt this is where they went. We should get the warrant to track the mother's phone tomorrow. Hopefully, that will lead us to them. Did the couple outside see anything?"

"They saw a black truck drive away, but that was it. The guy seems to think it was a Dodge."

Clay stepped outside. He felt the soft rain and cool breeze and looked out into the night, wondering where they were. Liberty and her mom had been in that room not more than an hour before.

Did the killer kidnap them? It was a large possibility. He could be taking them somewhere else to complete the job and dispose of their bodies. They were alive for the moment, but it wouldn't be for long. He had to find them soon.

CHAPTER TWENTY-FIVE

JJ drove south on Main Street until it turned into Perkins Road, and when she hit Highway 33, she headed west. It was a direction Liberty and her mother had traveled a lot when Liberty had been younger, but it had been years. Although the night diminished much of the landscape, the familiarity of the road crept in and sent Liberty back in time, and they weren't pleasant memories.

JJ's sister, Serene, lived in Langston, which was a small town on the outskirts of Oklahoma City. She lived with her husband, Joe, and they had no children.

Liberty was surprised that her mother was headed for her sister's after how the last visit had ended. JJ and Serene were fire and ice. If put in the same room, they were like hot grease spat from a skillet.

Liberty glanced at her mom as she drove. JJ's eyes drooped, her arms hanging lifelessly from the grip on the steering wheel.

"Mom, are you okay to drive? Do you want me to?"

She shook her head. "No, baby, I got it." She smiled and refocused on the road. She wiped the sweat away from her scalp with a shaky hand. She needed her high again.

"Just let me know if you do."

JJ nodded.

Liberty tilted her head against her door and let her eyelids shut. The image of her mother holding onto the steering wheel, forcing herself to stay awake and sober enough to get them to their destination safely, resonated in her thoughts. It was a small moment of comfort. Those were rare lately but always a welcome event. They were the remnants of her mom before drugs had taken over, traits she knew her mom still had if JJ would only allow them to surface.

She drifted to sleep in seconds and wandered into a recurring nightmare.

SHE WAS SIX YEARS OLD again, and it was Christmas Eve. Pete was storming down the hall toward Liberty's room to teach her a lesson about putting tape on the list, and her mother was in his way.

After a loud thud, the door to Liberty's room cracked.

Liberty closed her eyes and pleaded with the Lord. "Please, Heavenly Father. I know it's late. I don't know if you're listening, but I need you *real* bad." She cried hard, composed herself, then continued. "My mommy needs you. Please save her. Save me too. I don't know what he'll do—" More tears and sobs. "He needs to stop. Please stop him! Give my mommy strength. *Please!*"

Another giant *crash* against the wall. Liberty expected to see their bodies fly through the drywall, but it held. More violent sounds reached her ears as they wrestled. She heard slapping, stomps on the floor, two more thuds against the wall, and one against her door. It nearly busted apart this time.

"You *bastard*." JJ's voice was filled with venom. "I want you out of this house!"

"I ain't leavin'. I pay for this house!"

"Oh no? You're not leaving? We'll see about that."

Liberty heard feet stomping away.

"Where're you goin'? I'm talkin' to you, woman!"

"And I'm talkin' to you!" she screamed, and Liberty heard rapid footsteps.

Pete gasped. "What the hell?"

"I want you *gone*. Leave this house! I never want to see your ugly face again!"

There was a hollow *thunk*. Liberty would later learn that it had been the sound of an aluminum baseball bat hitting his head.

"Fuck! Shit, woman. You're crazy! Crazy! I don't know why I came back. You're a freakin' nut case. You and your bitch daughter!"

Then a louder *thunk* sounded.

Pete screamed. Then he stomped off, screeching in pain.

"Good riddance," JJ said in a low voice. That was the last they'd seen of Pete.

LIBERTY HAD SLEPT FOR twenty minutes, but it'd only felt like two. The car hit a bump, and it startled her awake. She sat up and looked around. She wasn't six anymore, and she wasn't in her bed. She was in a car with her mom. A line of golden light shone over the peaks of the mountains behind them and turned the black of night to a dark shade of blue.

"Are we almost there?" Liberty asked.

"Do you know where we're going?"

"It's been a long time, but yes. I'm surprised you're going there."

"Well... we need somewhere to go. Even if I only get as far as the front door. I'm not sure she'll let me in."

Liberty remembered the last time they'd been at Serene's house. JJ had left rehab early and had come by to pick up Liberty, who'd been staying with Joe and Serene while JJ was in treatment. Upset with her aunt's strict house rules, Liberty was relieved to go with her mom. Then, JJ and Serene started an argument that fueled so hot it almost turned physical. It had ended with Serene demanding they both leave her house.

Liberty would never forget the baleful look on Serene's face as she said, "You are not my sister. I don't want to ever see your face again!"

Serene had glanced at Liberty, said nothing, then slammed her front door.

JJ looked at the dashboard. "Shit."

Liberty looked across her mom at the gas gauge. The needle was touching the empty line. They drove the rest of the way through the town of Langston on fumes. JJ parked the car along the curb in front of Serene's house. Liberty saw doubt and tribulation in her mom's eyes as she looked at the two-story home.

JJ turned to her daughter. "This is a bad idea."

"Too late. We're here." Liberty shrugged nonchalantly.

"I thought you didn't like this place."

"I don't," Liberty said and exited the car. "But this should be interesting."

"I guess I don't have to like it either."

JJ groaned as she stepped out then slammed her door. She followed Liberty to the entrance, opened the screen, raised her fist to knock, then paused. She closed her eyes, took a deep breath, let it out, and rapped her knuckles on the wood. They waited a few minutes then heard movement and footsteps from inside. The footfalls got louder as they approached the door, then they stopped. The door didn't open.

"I knew this was a bad idea." She nodded to Liberty. "She's already seen who it is."

At that moment, the door opened halfway, and Serene stood in the open gap. She wore a heavy robe, and her bloodshot eyes wandered over them with a stern look. There was no smile, no surprise, and no welcome. She'd gained more weight since Liberty had last seen her, perhaps thirty pounds.

JJ broke the silence. "Sis."

Serene said nothing. She glared at JJ then turned her eyes to Liberty and forced a half smile.

"Aunt Serene."

A male voice called out from further in the house, "Who is it, Serene?"

Serene took a deep breath and answered, "The drug addict! Who else?" She turned and walked away from the open door. Under her breath, she added, "And now murderer."

JJ looked away. Her shoulders sank, and her body hunched as if someone had punched her in the gut. But the door remained open, so JJ motioned for Liberty to enter, and then she followed Liberty in.

Serene stopped at the foot of the stairs and faced them in the foyer. "I can't have you here." She shook her head. "The cops have already been by three times. I see them pass out front constantly. Like me, they know you'll eventually end up here. I can't help."

"I just want to talk. Five minutes." JJ stared at her. "Alone. Please."

Surrendering, Serene nodded and motioned JJ to follow her into the kitchen. "Liberty, you can take a seat in the front room, dear."

Her husband, Joe, stood halfway down the stairs and looked at Liberty. His eyes brightened, and his lips spread into a warm smile. "Hey, Liberty!"

"Hi, Joe." She smiled back. She'd always liked Joe. He was kind and good to her. Joe had made living with her aunt bearable.

"COFFEE?" SERENE OFFERED as she crossed the kitchen to the steaming pot. It had been preset the night before, so the coffee was ready.

"Please. Black." JJ locked her jaw as if preparing a mental guard.

Serene poured two cups.

"Sober?" Serene asked.

"For the moment."

Serene handed her a cup. "At least you're honest."

"Always am," JJ said.

Serene rolled her eyes.

"I didn't kill anybody, if that's what you're wonderin'."

"It doesn't matter. What matters is you've got Liberty in this mess. You continue to use and live in this world of crime, drug dealers, and murderers. What kind of life is that for your *daughter*?"

JJ's eyes narrowed, and she opened her mouth to say something but relented. She sighed. "You're right. That's why I'm here."

The words hit Serene unexpectedly. She couldn't recall the last time JJ had admitted that Serene was right. *This is a first.*

CHAPTER TWENTY-SIX

Serene and Joe whipped up scrambled eggs, bacon, and toast, and the home-cooked meal settled Liberty's appetite and taste buds. As her body began to digest the food, exhaustion overwhelmed her. Her head was cloudy and buzzed with a million thoughts, and although she worried her anxiety would keep her from sleeping, she knew she had to try. Her body needed to rejuvenate.

"Come on, Liberty," Joe said. "We got your room ready. Serene's upstairs puttin' some towels on your bed. You can use one to shower with, then get some rest. Looks like you could use some." He smiled.

"Thanks. A shower does sound good." Liberty stood up from the table.

JJ thumbed through their morning newspaper while nibbling on a burnt piece of toast.

"Unless you want to shower first, Mom," Liberty said.

"No. You go on. I'm gonna stretch out on the couch down here and catch some sleep. You got a spare blanket or two?" JJ asked Joe.

"Yeah, we got some blankets. I'll pull a couple outta the closet for ya."

JJ stopped Liberty. "I love you." JJ wore a slight smile with warmth in her eyes.

"Love you more," Liberty answered.

JJ's purse sat on a chair in the living room. Liberty took a quick peek to make sure her mom wasn't watching then dug through it. She found her phone and charger, which JJ had taken away, before trotting upstairs.

The warm shower washed away the film of dirt, grime, and sweat that covered her from head to toe. The water also comforted her nervous muscles and helped rinse out some of the hell she'd been through.

Flashes of the attacker in their house, falling on their upturned coffee table, flew through her head. She saw his spasming body, him gagging on blood, and dots of crimson splattering the carpet from his coughs. She also saw the three men tossing the baggy of drugs out to her from their sports car. *Are they dead too?* They'd been alive not twelve hours ago. She pictured their bloody bodies lying dead on the ground somewhere with lifeless eyes. She smelled the musty scent of their motel room and the fresh rain as they'd stepped out, repacked the car, and tore out of there. *Is there really a killer after us?* The thought was unbelievable and frightening.

She dried herself off with the towel her aunt had left her. The thick material was soft and smelled of fresh fabric softener.

She crossed the hall and entered her room. It was the same as she remembered except for some new additions. Several boxes were stacked in one corner, and a dusty treadmill took over a good portion of it. Serene had told her not to worry about all that stuff. She would get it moved soon so her room wasn't so packed. *Get it moved soon?* Liberty wondered how long her aunt expected her to stay.

She threw on a simple shirt and a comfortable pair of shorts to sleep in, then plugged in her phone, which was dead. Once it had some charge in it, she turned it on and wasn't surprised to see the list of texts from the officer, Clay, asking where she was, if she was okay, and pleading with her to give up their whereabouts.

You don't have to tell me where you are if you don't want to. Just tell me you guys are okay.

Did he take you? If you get a moment, dial 911 and keep it on speaker. We know he came to your motel.

Those words shook her body like a shockwave.

Did he take you? We know he came to your motel.

Reality set in. There really *was* a killer after them. She suddenly felt ill. She also felt sad for Clay. He genuinely cared for her, and he had no clue if she was alive or dead. She asked herself whether that was a good or bad thing. She shook her head. It was definitely a bad thing.

She texted a reply. *We are safe. No one has us.*

His reply came in a matter of seconds. *Thank God. Liberty? You're okay?*

Yes. We're okay, she texted.

You must have left right before he got there. Someone is watching out for you. Where are you now? I can find you, bring you both in, and protect you. You and your mother will be safe, I promise.

Liberty hesitated before responding. *I can't tell you. Not right now. I'm going to get some rest. We'll talk later.*

She set the phone down on the nightstand, crawled under her covers, and pulled them to her chin. She closed her eyes until her phone dinged. Curiosity won out, and she picked up her phone again.

I know a center that can help your mom. I talked to them. They'll admit your mom and get her the help she needs. I know a couple of the counselors there, and they are the best. She'll be in good hands. We just have to bring you both in and clear up this mess. I need to get you two safe. You are not safe yet, no matter where you are.

Her mind tossed back and forth. She wanted so badly to tell him where they were, but she couldn't. Not yet. She chose to sleep on it and decide when she woke up. Her eyes were sore, and she needed to rest. She put the phone on silent and surrendered to slumber.

SHE SLEPT HEAVILY, and toward the end, a dream crept in. It was a mix of disturbing memories and recent events. It started as all her nightmares did. Christmas Eve at six years old, the fighting outside, the pounding on the door, and Licorice barking. Then, there was silence. Tension was high. Licorice stayed facing the door like a guard but ceased barking.

Suddenly, the wooden door burst open with a loud *crack* as Pete kicked it in. He stepped inside. Shadows covered his exterior except for the glowing red eyes and the shimmer of the blade he held in his hand. It was the same knife the drug dealer had used in his attack.

Licorice was gone. No bark, no fight, just gone. Disappeared.

The evil man with the demon eyes slowly walked toward her, knife raised. "Bad girl." His voice was low, inhuman. "You didn't put it on the *list*!"

Liberty's eyes flew open, and her body shuddered. She was in her room at Aunt Serene's house. It had been a nightmare, the worst her subconscious had ever delivered. She shook the dream away and sat up.

The room was bright with sunlight. She looked at the time on her phone. She was surprised to find she'd slept for three and a half hours. There were four new texts from Officer Baxter, all trying to convince her to turn themselves in.

She ignored the texts, relieved herself in the bathroom, then sauntered downstairs to see her mother. She stepped into the living room to find an empty couch. A blanket was folded nicely at one end, and a pillow sat on top of it. *Where is Mom?*

Her heart stuttered, but she remained calm. Her mom was awake somewhere. Maybe in the bathroom or outside smoking.

Liberty crossed to the window and peeked out. Their beat-to-shit car was gone. She hurried to the kitchen, where she found Serene cutting vegetables. A game show was playing on the small TV on the counter.

"Hi, Liberty. Did you sleep well?"

"Where's Mom?"

"Your mom?" Serene averted her eyes. She commenced slicing carrots.

Liberty furrowed her brow. Heart racing, she asked again, "Where is she?" Liberty's tone was stern.

Serene took a deep breath and turned to her with her eyebrows up-turned. "You better sit down, honey."

"I don't want to sit down! Where is she?" she demanded, and Serene surrendered.

"She's gone."

"*You* did this."

"No. No, I didn't."

"Yes, you did! We both know you don't like my mom. You kicked her to the curb! I can't believe you did this to *me*!" Liberty spun and marched out. She pounded her feet upstairs.

"Liberty!" Serene called after her.

Liberty grabbed her phone from the nightstand and called her mom.

It went straight to voice mail.

"Liberty." Serene's tone was soft. She stood in the doorway to her bedroom. "Please sit down. I'll explain."

"I don't want you to explain. You sent her away, and there is a killer after her. Did you know that? Now she has no one. You just *killed* my mom." She kept a furious, stony face but couldn't stop her lips from trembling. Her muscles twitched and jerked throughout her body as adrenaline pumped.

"I didn't ask her to go, and I didn't make her. She chose to. That's why she came here. She wanted you safe. She knew I'd take you in and you could stay here."

"Then you let her go? *Why?* They're going to kill her."

"She's going to turn herself in to the police. She went straight there."

"You really believed that?" Liberty shook her head. "My mom is going to turn herself in?"

"That's what she said. And yes, I believed her. For the first time, I think. She seemed different. In a good way. She wants you taken care of, that's all. I thought it best to give her a chance. If she doesn't turn herself in by the end of the day, Joe and I will go to the police."

Liberty grunted and dropped her face in her hands. "She'll be dead by then. You don't understand. The drug dealers hired someone to find her and kill her. *A professional!* He's already killed three men. My mom doesn't understand. All she knows and cares about is getting high. That's all."

Serene sighed. "She's going to be okay. I promise." She approached Liberty with open arms.

Liberty was shocked. Serene had never been one to give out hugs or affection. It was more common for Joe to do that.

"Come on," Serene said, coaxing.

As angry as Liberty was, she knew her aunt's intentions were good. She didn't doubt the love Serene had for her, and Liberty really *needed* a hug. She fell into her arms, head on her aunt's chest. Serene held her tight as Liberty broke into sobs. They sat in that position for a few minutes until Liberty's breathing slowed to a regular pace, and she pulled back, wiping tears.

"Your mom is ill. She needs help," Serene said.

"No shit," Liberty said, and Serene gave a disapproving look. "Sorry. No crap."

"It's a disease. It runs in the family. You probably don't know much about our family, do you?"

Liberty shook her head. "No. Just you, really. And there's a cousin I met a couple of times. Grandma died when I was young, and I never met my grandpa."

Serene sighed, and her eyes turned away from Liberty as if looking into the past. "Our father was an alcoholic. He was very strict, and he had a list of rules. He posted them on the fridge. If you broke any of them, the devil would come out. He beat us from time to time. First with spankings and then the belt. Your mother got it the worst. She was such a rebel. Our dad worked long hours, so most of the day, we could play and have fun as long as our chores were done first. But when he came home... we were terrified of hearing his truck pull in. We didn't know what to expect. We could have all of our chores finished, no rules broken, house clean, dinner ready, and yet, if he had a bad day at work, he'd still take it out on us. And Mom."

"What about Grandma? What did she do?"

"Nothing. She didn't try to stop him. She sat in the background like a beaten dog. Don't get me wrong. She was a great mom when he wasn't around. But when he was home, she was distant. She thought we deserved the punishment too. After all, we did break the rules. She really got most of the beatings though. Probably more abuse than I know of. It wasn't until later that I realized she had a drinking problem too. She'd been drinking the whole time. Who could blame her? Our childhood was a nightmare.

"Our dad died of a heart attack when I turned twenty. I thought that once he was gone, mom would be different. That she'd apologize for the hell she allowed us to go through. But she never did. Five years after our dad died, cancer took her away."

It struck Liberty then why her mother had fought so hard to keep Pete from hurting her. Because Grandma had never done that for JJ.

"That's how bad this disease is. It's taken away so many people." Serene's tone was melancholic.

"I don't know if Mom will accept any help," Liberty said.

"I know. She's a mule. That's another thing that runs rampant in this family. I tried for so many years. I almost had her back. I still see glimpses of the Jemma I knew, but those moments are fewer and fewer. It's you I really worry about. I hope you don't hate me. I'm not trying to take you away from your mom, and that's the truth. The environment you're in frightens me, and I worry what road you'll go down."

"Trust me. It's a road in the opposite direction."

Serene grinned. "You're such a bright girl—young lady, I should say."

"Where did all of this start with my mom? She wasn't always like this."

"No, she wasn't. She had a bright future. She always got good grades in high school and received a Pell Grant to move on to college. She even planned to major in psychology. Then she got pregnant with you from a man she'd just broken up with. I guess they'd been dating awhile, but I never met him. He'd disappeared without knowing you were coming. She worked two jobs and took online classes for a while. I helped when I could and watched you while she worked. The addiction didn't start until she hooked up again with a former boyfriend who had just come back from the war. Do you remember Pete?"

Flashes of that monster outside her door came to mind. Liberty nodded. "How could I forget?"

"No, how could you? He was a reprehensible asshole."

"Aunt Serene?" Liberty raised her eyebrows at her aunt's curse word.

Serene shrugged, and they shared a chuckle. "Sorry. I couldn't find a lesser word to describe him. What he did was enough to cause ir-reversible damage. That last night in your house, when they had that horrible fight—" She paused, took a deep breath, and continued. "He broke her arm in three places. She had to have a cast and pins in her arm. She had to have surgery for internal bleeding and received fif-teen stitches above her right eye. She nearly lost sight in that eye. If his blows had been less than a quarter of an inch lower, she would have. I'm stunned how she fought him off. A blood-caked eye she couldn't see out of and a broken arm—how did she wield that bat and smack him with it? And hard enough to crack his skull and send him running?" She shook her head.

"She was in so much pain," Serene continued. "Her doctor pre-scribed pain medicine, Percocet, and he continued to refill them for months. She got hooked. She was downing ten to fifteen pills a day. Finally, the doctor pulled back and stopped refilling, but it was too late. And like I said, addiction runs in the family. She was successful for a short while in getting other doctors to write prescriptions. When the scripts stopped, she moved to street pills until they got too expensive, and it became harder and harder to get them. Heroin on the streets is cheap. It was the alternative she needed. It's gotten worse ever since."

Serene's eyes fell to the floor. "I never imagined it'd come to this. What you two have been through... that attack... I just can't wrap my brain around it. It's beyond my comprehension. I don't know what will happen to her. But I know my sister is tough."

Liberty remained silent for a moment as she stared at the floor. "I don't get it. We're in this together, and we should both surrender to the police. She didn't go to them. She went to get drugs." Tears ran from her eyes. "She chose drugs over me. Again."

"Oh, honey," Serene said and pressed Liberty's head to her chest again.

Liberty didn't resist. "I thought that... I don't know," Liberty mumbled. "That she'd changed a little, or this would get her to see differently. I guess I'm the fool."

"You are not the fool. You love your mother, and there's no crime in that. We're all guilty of it. All I know is, this is not your mother. It is the drugs. She does love you, and tonight, she made the toughest choice in her life. Liberty, she admitted how dependent she's been on you and how selfish she's been. It was not easy for her to let you go."

"So she asked you to take me in?"

"Yes. She planned to leave while you were asleep because she knew you wouldn't let her leave. I gave her some cash to get gas and food. I've never seen her so heartbroken."

Liberty sat up. "I know. She's stupid for doing it. It's going to get her killed."

"The police will protect her, honey."

"If she turns herself in." She thought about the texts from Clay. If JJ had turned herself in, Liberty would have heard by now. "But I know she hasn't."

Serene sighed.

"We have to go find her." Liberty stood up and grabbed her backpack. Permission or not, she was leaving.

Serene stood, blocking the doorway. "Liberty, we can't. We're not going after her. Give her a chance to turn herself in."

"You're not getting it, Aunt Serene."

"No, *you're* not getting it. I'm not letting you go."

Heat rose in Liberty's face, and her mind raced through a thousand alternatives. Finally, she threw her backpack to the ground. "Fine."

CHAPTER TWENTY-SEVEN

Three hours after the sun went down, so did Serene and Joe. They watched TV after dinner until close to eleven, then Serene switched the screen off and called it a night. They hadn't contacted the police like promised. No word had come that JJ had turned herself in. When confronted by Liberty, Serene promised she would go to the police first thing in the morning. Liberty had to play along for her plan to work, so she agreed with Serene without a fuss.

Liberty plodded sleepily to her room, and they went to theirs. An hour and a half went by with no sound. Liberty felt it safe enough to make her move.

She slipped out of bed, quickly changed into pants and a shirt, unzipped her bag, stuffed her pajamas in, and checked the gun. It was a sleek black pistol. Light glimmered off its steel, and it was heavy in her hand.

Joe always kept a loaded pistol in the nightstand next to his bed for protection. Years before, when Liberty had stayed there, she'd gotten to know Joe and Serene well. She'd memorized their habits, knew where they kept things, and fortunately for her, Joe hadn't changed his ways.

While the two had been downstairs preparing dinner, she'd taken the opportunity to sneak into their bedroom. She'd approached the nightstand quickly and quietly. There was a keyhole on the drawer, which he'd always kept locked. Joe had a love for guns and had taken her to a range a couple of times and taught her how to shoot. Liberty had tried once before to steal the gun and run away. She'd never managed either.

That time, to her surprise, she pulled on the drawer, and it opened with ease. *Unlocked.* Perhaps he felt safe enough knowing there weren't any children in the house and hadn't thought to secure it.

The gun lay beneath a pile of socks. She lifted the pistol in one hand and ejected the cartridge. It was full of bullets. She pushed the cartridge back in quietly until it snapped into place, and she made sure the safety was on. She hurried back to her room and hid it in her bag. The rest of the day and night she'd remained on a high alert, afraid he would find the pistol gone, and it would ruin her plans of escape.

With Joe and Serene asleep, Liberty zipped up her bag and crept out of her room. She stepped into the hallway, and the floor cried under her foot with a loud creak. Wincing, she froze and listened for any movement from their room, but none came. She continued down the hall. She forced her brain to remember where on the floor not to step, like Indiana Jones avoiding the spots that would trigger a poisonous dart or a swinging blade.

She kept close to the wall and made it to the edge of the stairwell without a sound. The stairs were another thing altogether. They groaned like an old man's frail bones. She took them slowly and as lightly as she could and made it to the bottom floor without alarm.

She crossed into the kitchen, where the key rack hung on the wall. They had two vehicles. One was a Mazda 6 parked in the garage, and the other was a Ford Escape in the driveway outside. She picked the Escape so she didn't have to open a noisy garage or move a vehicle to get out.

Once inside the Escape, she turned the key enough to move the gear into neutral while keeping her foot on the brake pedal. She didn't want to start the engine and awaken them. The driveway was inclined, so gravity should have moved the vehicle backward on its own. She let go of the brake, but it wasn't budging. *What am I missing? Parking brake!* She quickly found the handle and disengaged it. The vehicle rolled fast, and she turned the steering wheel to her right.

The small SUV bumped over the gutter and was heading for a parked car across the street. Liberty quickly slammed on the brake, and it rocked to a stop two feet away from impact. She took a deep breath and let it out.

She tilted the rearview mirror to adjust for her lack of height and studied her situation. She wanted to move the Escape farther away before starting the engine and quickly gauged a solution. She cranked the steering wheel left and released the brake. The vehicle moved past the parked car then rolled another thirty feet until she stopped it. She turned the engine over. It was surprisingly quiet, and although the brakes were extremely touchy and took a while to get accustomed to, she found the Escape to be much easier to drive than their van was. She adjusted her seat, put the car in gear, and drove away.

Liberty had a good idea of where her mother had gone. They had packed their camping gear in case they had to use it. There was only one place her mother would go. JJ's favorite spot, Lake McMurtry. Liberty set the GPS in her phone to guide her.

CHAPTER TWENTY-EIGHT

Jon stood outside his hotel room on the second floor, looking out at the drizzling night. The rain had come back but without the winds and threat of tornadoes. Its fresh, spring scent was delicious to his senses, and it comforted him to watch nature and take in its beauty. It was perhaps the only thing that calmed the vicious beast in him.

He tipped the beer bottle back and took a gulp. He didn't drink much, and when he did, he kept it down to no more than two or three beers. As a soldier, he needed to keep his senses sharp. He had a mission to complete, and he couldn't risk it being thwarted because of stupidity or intoxication. Tonight, there would be no tracking and no bloodshed. He wanted JJ and Liberty to settle in, get comfortable, and be off guard.

He knew where they'd gone. They were out of money. That was easy to figure out. Even if it had only been a couple of years, he knew JJ's habits from living with her before. He also knew the life of a junkie, which was what she had become.

They'd stayed two nights in a dumpy motel because it was cheap, and she'd spent very little on her heroin. He'd learned that from questioning Sal. She should have bought more—she *needed* more. Jon counted on that. He would use it to his advantage.

Laughter broke his concentration, and he turned toward its source. Three young guys and a lady stumbled to their room three doors down from his. The woman had long hair that draped down her back, and she was in a tank top and hideous skirt. Her outfit didn't match the weather. The skirt was short enough to catch the wrong kind of attention.

She stumbled against the railing and almost went over it, and all four of them broke out into laughter. They were intoxicated and loud.

The woman caught Jon's gaze, locked onto his eyes, and pulled a seductive smile. "Heeey! You wanna paaarty? 'Cause we're havin' a party in our room." Her words came out slurred, and she laughed again. Her friends appeared reluctant to invite him, as if Jon might be a threat.

"No thanks." Jon turned away and took another swig of beer.

"I wanna beer," the lady called out to him. "C-Can I have a beer?"

"We have some in the room, Candy," one of the men said while another one worked on getting their door open. He struggled to insert the card into the slot.

"But I want one of his," she demanded, pointing her finger. "He's got good shit. I can tell."

Jon closed his eyes for a second and focused on the patter of the rain to calm himself. He needed to avoid a situation, and he already teetered on the edge of imploding due to his thoughtless mistakes at the motel. He had been so close to catching them. And he should have killed that couple who had entered the office. In his rearview mirror, he had seen the lady's reaction as she'd looked down at his handiwork. He was sure they had called the cops, and they'd probably seen his truck drive away. They would have told the police that.

Dammit! Now I'm going to have to dump my truck. He tightened his grip around the bottle, wanting to crush it.

Tension cut the air. This small group was extremely high, and although giddy then, the woman didn't appear to have the sense enough to filter her thoughts or words. She wobbled over to him like a newborn fawn learning to walk for the first time then leaned an elbow on the railing close by. She glanced behind Jon and eyed the four beers sitting in a Styrofoam carton of ice.

"Hey, cowboy." She laughed. "How 'bout one a dem beers?"

"Come on, Candy." One of the other men continued to pull her away from Jon. "We got our own inside."

"You got *shit*! He's got that imported stuff. It'sss good."

She was right. Hoegaarden was a personal favorite beer of his, and he could only find it in select stores. It was an imported beer from Curacao that carried the aroma of orange peel, coriander, and herbs. He could afford to give her one, but it wasn't in his nature.

"No," Jon answered her and said nothing more.

Her mouth dropped open, and she gave him a strange look. "You got four there. I juuust want one. You can give up one. We'll give you two of ours for it. Come on."

Jon kept his gaze forward. *Come on, Jon. You don't need this.* He knew it would bring unwanted, dangerous attention. Maybe even cops. Bodies were already stacking up. He just wanted the drunk woman to drop it and go away, but she was the type that wasn't going to give up.

One of her friends stepped up to Jon. "How much? I'll pay you for it." He had an apology in his eyes for Candy's behavior.

"I said no." Jon tipped his beer again.

"Fucker," she said.

"*Candy!*" her friend yelled at her then turned back to Jon. "Just to shut the bitch up, man. Just one, please. I'll pay."

He could kill them all and dispose of their bodies in under two minutes. He wanted to. The dark desire deep in his gut that fed his evil actions called out to him. It whispered in his ear. His training taught him not to listen to temptation. It was not the time to kill. That could be the stupid mistake that took him down, and his mission was essential. Getting to JJ and Liberty was much more important.

"Just walk away," he warned them.

"Come on, asshole!" The man was getting upset. "One beer."

"Lissssten," Candy slurred to Jon. "I got three big guys here with me. Plus, I'm one mean bitch. Get it? I'm takin' one."

She bent down, reaching for a beer. Jon finished the last swallow, gripped the neck of the bottle, turned, then smashed it against the back of her head. The bottle glanced off her skull with a sickening thud, and her body fell to the ground. The men stood stunned, and Jon acted faster than their drunken reactions could.

Jon leaped over her body, landed, then snapped a front kick to one man's gut, folding him in half. Jon entangled his fingers in the same guy's hair and pulled his head back so he could smack his nose with an open palm.

Candy rolled on the ground, whimpering and cussing while holding her bleeding head.

Finally, another man attacked.

Jon sidestepped him, grabbed the back of his head, and slammed his face against the railing, breaking his nose. He spun again and thrust a side kick into the next incoming chest, sending the man smashing against the wall. He turned back to Broken Nose and hit his throat with the side of his palm.

Candy jumped onto his back and began clawing his bare arms with her nails and pulling at his hair. The other man he had front kicked jumped in again, swinging a fist. He connected a couple of good punches to Jon, but it didn't faze him.

Disregarding the wild cat on his back for the moment, Jon retaliated with a blur of punches to the man's face and solar plexus. Then he twisted, crouched, and brought his right arm between Candy's legs as his left grabbed the back of her hair.

Using the leverage of his right arm under her and his left hand to guide, he flung Candy over his head, toppling onto the other man.

He crouched over the woman and gripped her throat in his hand, squeezing it. Her eyes bulged, and she gawked, trying but unable to bring in air. He was losing it. At that moment, he *wanted* to kill. The tension of not accomplishing his task with JJ and Liberty consumed him, and he was releasing it on this group.

The man he'd side-kicked recovered and charged him with a loud cry as he knocked Jon back off the woman. They wrestled, but Jon escaped and shot back up to his feet. The other man grabbed his shirt in one hand, ready to pummel Jon with the other fist. Jon reached over, grabbed the hand that held him, and twisted it quickly, resulting in several snaps. The man instantly fell to his knees, shrieking.

Broken Nose came out of nowhere, swinging a fire extinguisher. Jon stepped toward him and blocked the arm that held the weapon. Then he snapped a back elbow into the man's busted nose, spattering blood.

Jon took the fire extinguisher and smacked the head of the man already on the ground, flattening him. He turned his attention to the woman and the last man, both lying on the cement, and kicked their ribs, arms, and legs in a fit of rage.

He stood over them, dropped the extinguisher, and wiped spittle from his mouth while breathing heavily. That had not been the fight of a trained professional but of an enraged drunk.

The night was silent and still. Their commotion hadn't brought unwanted attention yet. Three of the four opponents squirmed in pain on the ground. The guy he'd hit with the extinguisher was out cold. It was possible that Jon had killed him.

He took the key card out of the man's hand, opened their room, then one by one, threw them in. He shut the door and left them alone. He *wanted* to take his knife and cut them. The desire to finish their weak bodies was intense. The pit of his stomach cried for it, but he left before the desire took over. Later, he would thank himself for that.

Their drunkenness and pain should subdue them for hours. But he couldn't take a risk by staying there. It was unlikely, but one of them might be smart enough to sober up and call the police.

Jon grabbed his belongings and left the hotel. He would find a spot to park and catch a few winks in his truck before dawn.

CHAPTER TWENTY-NINE

Detective Clay Baxter searched Jemma and Liberty's home under the cover of darkness. He was alone and chose to turn on one lamp, which shed enough light for him to search for clues. He needed to find out where they'd gone. Texts and calls to Liberty had gotten him nowhere. He was positive she was comfortable with him and might divulge their whereabouts, but he suspected that her mother wouldn't allow her to.

He'd gotten the warrant to track the GPS on JJ's phone, but that had come up empty. If JJ had shut her phone down and removed its battery, there was nothing they could do. Clay was sure that was the case.

He would have to find Jemma and Liberty the old-fashioned way. There were clues in the house—he knew it. He just had to find them. He let his senses lead him. Clearing his mind, he let his heart be the guide.

He looked at their pictures again. Several of them had been taken near a lake where they'd camped. There was a tent, a firepit, and a picnic table in a couple of the shots. While searching through their rooms, he came across an empty closet—almost empty. There was a flashlight and a rolled-up tarp sitting in there, along with one unrolled sleeping bag. It was part of a camping-gear set. *But where is the rest?* He'd seen a tent in those pictures.

The empty spot next to the items in the closet had fibers of the carpet flattened out and dead pieces of grass. Something had been there. It had to have been the rest of their camping gear.

They'd taken the gear and planned on camping. Either they'd run out of money for motels, or the city had gotten too hot for the runaways. Or both. Where they'd gone to camp was still a mystery. According to the pictures, it was near a lake.

There were two famous recreational spots in Stillwater. There was Boomer Lake, or a little further out was Lake McMurtry. *Which one is it?* He wasn't much of a camper or fisherman himself, so he hadn't visited either of them enough to determine which one they'd been at in the pictures.

He'd sent two patrol cars to Boomer Lake—although they hadn't reported in yet—so that area was covered.

He jumped back in his vehicle and sped in the direction of Lake McMurtry.

CHAPTER THIRTY

"**H**ope"
I have seen you falling apart for a while now.

I kept holding onto hope... hope that you would get help and stop using...

Hope that we could have a normal life.

Now I hope and pray that you have finally hit rock bottom and will get clean.

Hope is all I have left.

-Poem from Liberty Justice's Diary

Liberty Justice arrived at the west entrance to McMurtry Lake Recreational Park in the dark of night. It was two in the morning, and there were several camp spots throughout the park. There was no way to find JJ in the black of night unless she went from tent to tent and knocked on each screen.

She *believed* her mother was there, somewhere deep within the grounds. She parked in the lot at the front entrance, turned the vehicle off, and stared at the stars and moon that peeked through a break in the storm clouds. The rain had subsided for the moment. She cracked the window to feel the cool breeze calm her anxious body.

Looking through the windshield at the starry sky, she let the mystery of space overwhelm her. There was so much to life she didn't know. It was hard to think of the future when the present in front of her eyes was a massive storm of chaos and fear. But looking up at the stars fed her curiosity of the unknown and the possibilities it held. It was hope. Hope there *was* a future for her life. One that involved a career of writing or the chance of finding a soul mate to share her life with. As much as she wanted to weave tales of wondrous places and people and create an escape for readers from the world of abandonment and pain, there was also a fear that she might never achieve that goal.

Fear sucked all her energy away. It was inescapable. The rain started again, pattering droplets against the windshield. The water entered her open window, so she closed it. The rumble of thunder in the distance followed by the flash of lightning raised memories of nights years ago. Sitting on the porch of a small house, eating watermelon, and watching the fireworks of a lightning storm with her mom. She remembered her mother wiping watermelon juice from the corner of her mouth and smiling down at her.

She craved moments like that. She wondered if they were all in the past, never to be visited again. Maybe she was living on memories and a fool's hope. Those questions plagued her but only for a moment. Her mother was worth the fight. Liberty was going to do whatever it took to win her back. If she could achieve that, she would win back the old memories as well as create new ones. She was determined, and her mother deserved that much.

On the other hand, she was aware that she might not accomplish saving her mother. She had to be okay with it. If she gave it 100 percent, she could live with that outcome. Maybe.

Thunder rumbled in the distance, and the clouds moved with the breeze. The moon and stars disappeared behind the clouds again, and she was left in darkness. Her eyelids were heavy. The weight of slumber pulled them down, and her thoughts drifted into dreams.

SHE AWOKE THE NEXT morning to the sun peeking over the mountains, and a cold chill filled the Escape. She sat up with an ache in her neck, which she rubbed to no avail. She turned the engine over and started the heat. It took a minute or two, but soon, the air came out hot and thawed her bones.

She looked around at the trees. The sign ahead let her know campgrounds lay within. The road split two ways, but her memory told her to drive to the right. JJ had her favorite spot. Liberty knew it was a ways in but couldn't remember exactly where. She would have to resort to her senses and look for the color of their tent to find it. She prayed she could.

It took just shy of fifteen minutes before she saw the right camping spot. The dirt drive opened and led to a grassy area next to the lake. It was spotted with a mix of pines and junipers as well as oak, redbud, and elm trees. The branches waved back and forth with the breeze underneath a gray sky, and bits of sun glanced through clouds. The blue lake provided the backdrop for the array of trees. In front of them was a firepit and a picnic table and, beyond that, a familiar yellow-and-brown dome. There was no mistaking the ugly tent. She'd never seen another of its kind. It bobbled back and forth against the wind, and her mother sat on the ground in front of the firepit with her legs crisscrossed. Her body was bent forward, and her long hair draped down, covering her face. Her lean body looked frail in the blue jeans and T-shirt. A glint of sunlight bounced off the nearly empty bottle of vodka next to her. She held a half-smoked cigarette in her right hand.

Liberty parked the Escape next to the beat-up Buick. As she approached her mother, she saw JJ's body shaking. Probably from withdrawals.

"Mom?" She stopped short of the firepit. Small flames bounced in its center and danced with the breeze.

JJ raised her head with all its heavy hair, her sunken, bloodshot eyes under swollen lids. No look of surprise came over them.

"Libeeerty?" Her voice slurred. "My Lib-Lib? What're you doing here?"

JJ hadn't called her that since she was a child.

"I came to get you."

"You're not s'posed to be here."

"Neither are you."

"Yesss, I am." JJ hung her head. "I'm right where I'm s'posed to be."

Her mom looked defeated. Although JJ had finished almost all of the vodka, Liberty knew that alcohol was no replacement for heroin. Her body still needed it.

"Are you out?" Liberty asked, meaning the drug. She sat down.

JJ nodded. "I couldn't find nobody to s-s-sell me any. They all heard what happened to the other guys. Sis gave me fifty bucks. I put ten in gas, which got me here on fumes." She chuckled.

She looked up at her daughter, regret plain in her eyes. "I'm sorry. I tried. I really tried. I didn't want to get high no more. It'sss not about getting high now. My body needs it or... or... it falls apart. I could diiiie. I juuust disappoint you. I know I do," she whined.

Liberty couldn't refute that but was sad anyway.

"I came here 'cause it's my happy place. You and I always had a good time here." She took a drag from her cigarette and blew the smoke out. "I bought vodka to at least numb my body. Maybe I won't feel the pain so much, you know?"

"What pain?"

"*What pain?*" JJ guffawed. "So much pain. I should be a better mom for you. You are so smart, sooo pretty. There's so much future out there for you, Lib-Lib. Please don't follow me. I'm only goin' to bring you down. Forgive me for what I did. I only did it for you. I know you don't like your aunt's, but it'sss the best place for you."

"She's not so bad," Liberty said.

"That's good. She's not a bad person. Means well. For the most part." She rolled her eyes. "At least you won't get hurt there."

"Mom, what the hell are you talking about? Are you that *stupid*?"

JJ sat up straight as if someone had pricked her butt with a pin.

"What makes you think that's better for me?" Liberty continued. "I'll make my own decisions, and I'll go down the path I want to take. One that's right for me, and it is certainly not the path you're on. I don't need to be apart from you to see that. But if you think for one second that I don't need you—" Liberty's lips trembled, and her eyes went red. "You are *dead wrong*. I *need* you."

"Oh, honey, that's not what I meant. It's juuust, I am sick. Don't you see? I ain't gettin' no better. Only worse. And that's not good for you."

"What's important is what's good for you. You need to get better."

"I know, sweetie." Her mother nodded. "I do, but I can't. I just can't beat this shit!" she said between sobs. Liberty noticed that she wasn't slurring her words as much. Perhaps her crying had sobered her a bit.

"Yes, you can. Not by yourself, but you can. There is help out there."

"Help?" she squawked. "I've tried help. Those places do good for a while, but I always find myself back here again."

"So you're just going to stop trying?" Liberty challenged. "Just give up? That's not the momma that raised me."

JJ sighed. "I have nothing left."

"You have me. Isn't that enough?" Liberty asked.

"You are worth that and more," JJ said. "Dammit, but this drug... this shit... it's all I live for. I am selfish, Liberty, because it's all I care about. It is all I crave. I get up in the morning, and it's the first thing on my mind. *How do I get it?* I spend my day figuring out where I'll get the money and who I'll buy from. Where do I go for the drop? Do I shoot it up there in the car, or will I have enough strength to get home and do it there? Then once it's worn off, do I have enough to get high again and get through the night? While I'm sleepin', I dream of it. It hovers over my head and shoulders like a black devil. It never lets me go, never lets me think of you, think of food, think of work, think of family or friends or nothin'. Don't you get it? It doesn't let me do anything but *crave* it and find new ways how to get it and shoot it. My whole day—every day—revolves around the world of heroin.

"It's the high I'm chasin', Lib. That high I got when I first tasted it. It was *so* damned good, I wanted to always feel that way. Bitch of it is, you never get that same high again. I hate to say it, Liberty, but you're not enough." Tears rolled from her eyes. "This shit's still more important." JJ shrugged.

Liberty saw the Road Runner Looney Tune in her head. The Road Runner stopped at the edge of the cliff while Wile E. Coyote continued to run past the edge and out into midair. Once he realized his mistake, he gave a frightful look, held up a sign that said Oops, and fell to the distant ground below. A small puff of dust blew up from his landing, then a large boulder fell, too, and smashed him farther into the ground. That was how Liberty felt hearing JJ's words.

It was no surprise to Liberty. She knew the drug was more important, but to hear it from her mom's own lips hurt. Real bad. She'd seen *Intervention* episodes on A&E a million times and had learned what heroin did to a person. She knew it was an addiction, a disease, a mind and body takeover. But dammit, that was her *mom*.

"It rained last night." JJ's words were somber. "Not heavy, just light rain. I sat out here in it. It felt good. Something so clean. Felt like it was bathing my body. This body doesn't deserve much. Not good, clean rain like that anyways. In the distance, I saw lightnin', and thunder followed. You know what I craved?" She looked up at Liberty with a sly grin.

"Watermelon," Liberty answered.

"Watermelon." Her smile widened and eyes glowed with the memory. "I loved those nights we'd sit on the porch eating watermelon and watching 'God paint the sky with lightning bolts.' That's what you used to say, and I found it so poetic. I craved watermelon so bad last night, I could taste it. Then I asked myself *why*? It's not the watermelon, lightnin', and thunder I crave, although I love that combination. It's that moment I shared with you. It's the thought and hope for better days." Her eyes seemed to melt into Liberty's. "I *want* that too. I really do."

"I do, too, Mom. You can have it back. I can have my mom back if you just give it a try."

"No." She shook her head. "I can't go back to those places, Liberty. I just can't. They don't work. Don't you see? This is the end for me. I need you to go. Go and live the life I never got to."

"What are you talking about?"

JJ let out a deep breath and struggled to say the next words. She fiddled with the dirt by drawing circles in it with her finger then finally said, "I came here to die. That killer is going to find me here. It's just a matter of time. I'm goin' to continue to drink, and either I'll die from withdrawals, or I'll die from that killer they hired to find me. Then this whole nightmare will be over. You might miss me, though I can't imagine why, and you'll probably mourn me despite all I've done. But eventually, life will be better for you."

"Who the hell do you think you are?" Liberty demanded. "You got it all figured out? Tell me. Who does that really benefit? 'Cause it sure isn't me! You don't think my life will be messed up? You don't think I still need my mom? I'll tell you who that works out for. *You!* That's who, and no one else. You get to take the easy way out. Die and move on and leave me in this shit life to figure everything else out. Uncle Joe and Aunt Serene are not my mom. I only have one of those, and she better get her shit together and start being my mom again! You got that?"

JJ's body jerked backward as if an invisible force had smacked her. Her eyes widened, and her mouth went slack.

"You're going to turn yourself in, and we're going to straighten this whole thing out." Liberty waved her hands in the air, gesturing to the mess around them. "Because we didn't kill anybody. Then you are going straight into rehab." Liberty didn't want to tell her that she'd talked to the cops and they had a place set up for her. JJ would go nuts with that information. "Once you are in rehab, you are going to work the program."

"No, no, no, I am not!" JJ shook her head and gestured wildly.

"Oh yes, you are."

"You don't know a thing you're talkin' about."

"Yes, I do. You don't have a choice this time." Liberty was stern and on her feet, pointing at JJ. "You are *going* to work the program!"

"You don't make choices for me! I make my *own* choices! I am stayin' *right here*!" JJ's face bloomed red.

"No, you're not! You are coming with me. You are not going to *die*!" Liberty withdrew the pistol from her coat, and JJ's eyes widened. "If that asshole comes anywhere near you, I'm shooting him full of holes. Got it? But you are not going to die! I won't let you. Even if I have to shoot you, and I will. I will shoot you in the leg or arm but not anywhere that will kill you. I'm not letting you off that easy."

For the first time in a long time, JJ was empty of words. Her shoulders sank, and she let out a puff of air, and her face seemed to unclench. She held a small stick in her hand that she fidgeted with before throwing it into the fire.

"I guess I got no choice," JJ said.

"No, you don't." Liberty plopped down on a stump next to the firepit across from her mom. "So, what do you have for breakfast?" Liberty asked casually, and JJ's face brightened.

"Breakfast?" She moved her head back and forth as if looking for items, then she picked up the bottle of vodka and shook it. "This is it, babe."

"Ugh." Liberty rolled her eyes. "We should still have some eggs in the cooler. I can boil some."

Liberty held the gun down at her side, and JJ nodded at it.

"Where'd you get that?"

"Uncle Joe keeps one in his nightstand."

"Really? Since when?"

"Since forever. He had it when I stayed with them while you were at the hospital."

JJ set the bottle down. "Hospital? That was a long time ago."

"That's where it all started, didn't it?"

"Started? What do you mean?"

"Aunt Serene said it was the pain pills prescribed to you during that time that started this addiction."

"Aunt Serene said that?" JJ blurted. "What the hell does *she* know? And why did she bring that up? Why would she tell you that?"

"Because she's concerned about you."

"Concerned about me? That's a new one. You two talkin' about me? What to do with this mess of a woman."

Liberty instantly regretted bringing her aunt up. "It wasn't like that."

"*Sure.* What else did she say?"

"Nothing I didn't already know. But it makes sense if that's when it all started."

"Sort of," JJ agreed. The vodka in JJ's system seemed to have loosened her tongue. "I always had tendencies to alcohol, pot, coke—whatever got me high. I was a bit of a partier. Addiction lurked behind everything, waiting for the curtain to pull back and let it onstage. I knew once it happened, there'd be no turnin' back. When I was sent to the hospital by that worthless asshole, Pete, it was the tippin' point. Like I fell off the ledge I'd been dancin' on and into this dark pit, and I just can't climb my way out anymore."

"Yes, you can."

JJ's eyes looked up to meet Liberty's without raising her head. "But I don't want to."

"You don't *want* to?" Liberty scrunched her face. "You just said earlier that—"

"I know what I said. I'm also a liar, a manipulator, and not just to you, but to m'self. Just bein' honest."

A wave of disappointment shook Liberty's body.

"I'm sorry, babe. It's just the way it is. I'll fix us some eggs, and then you better scooch. You shouldn't be here." She half smiled then stood up to get the eggs.

They remained silent as JJ rummaged through the trunk of the car. Liberty's head spun with too many thoughts to process.

JJ withdrew a pot and outstretched it to Liberty. "Wanna take this and get some water to boil?"

Liberty snatched it out of her hand.

"Follow that path. It should take you to the restrooms and a water fountain. You can fill the pot there."

Liberty sauntered down the trail, thinking to herself. *Even if I make her get help, if she doesn't want it, no amount of rehab will ever work.*

CHAPTER THIRTY-ONE

It took longer than Liberty anticipated to reach the restrooms and water fountain. Fifteen minutes in, she was questioning if she'd taken the wrong path. Then she turned a corner, and there were the restrooms, sitting among trees. It was a square, brown-painted building with women and men symbols painted in white. In front of it was a drinking fountain with a spigot poking out of its side.

She bent her head down and shot cold water into her mouth. Some of it missed and splashed down the front of her shirt, but it was refreshing. She crouched and turned the faucet on to fill the pot.

Once she stood and turned to walk back, she heard rustling leaves and twigs snapping. She twisted around and rested her right hand on the pistol in the back of her pants. An outline of a figure approached through the oak trees, and her hair stood on end. *Run or stay put? Draw the pistol or wait?* She couldn't decide, so she froze, every nerve aware.

She saw the white of a button-down shirt followed by blue jeans and a shiny object set on the belt but not where the buckle should be. It was farther down his waist, almost on his hip. It was a badge.

The officer saw her and stopped. He put his hands up in front of him to assure her that he was a friend and not to bolt. "Liberty?"

"Don't move. You stay right there," Liberty warned with a shaky tone. She didn't draw her gun but kept her hand on it.

"It's okay, Liberty. It's me. Detective Clay Baxter." His face softened. "I'm the one who's been talking to you. Well, texting you, that is."

Liberty didn't know what to think. She kept her stance. She hadn't prepared herself to meet Clay. Her eyes darted back and forth.

"I'm alone. I'm just glad I found you." He smiled. "I've been combing this place for hours. Are you okay? Is your mom all right?"

"How do I know you're Clay?" she asked. *What if it is the killer? Or another officer, posing?*

"You are one of a very few I've told about my past and who my mom is—what she did to get drugs and what it did to me. Beyond a therapist and a close friend, I haven't told anyone."

Her shoulders relaxed. She took a deep breath but didn't release her grip on the gun.

"You're safe with me, Liberty. I am here to help."

"I just... I just don't know if my mom is ready. I don't know if I am." A cry crept into her voice.

"When is anyone ever ready? I just want to protect you and your mom. The killer is still out there." He slowly walked toward her, dropping his hands.

Liberty stared at the ground, contemplating.

"Let's get you and your mother safe. Then we'll figure it out from there." He stopped three feet short of her and raised his eyebrows. "Okay?"

She shuffled backward and put a warning hand out to him. "Stop right there. Don't come any closer."

CHAPTER THIRTY-TWO

Jon sat in a group of trees and watched as JJ set a carton of eggs down on a flat rock next to the fire. The flames dwindled and were about to die. JJ took a large log and placed it in the coals then set another smaller log against it. The fire licked at the underside of them.

Jon had watched Liberty march up the hill moments before. The daughter was out of sight then, and Jon had the mother all to himself.

JJ lifted the bottle, appeared to contemplate, then set it down. Her hands trembled, and Jon saw beads of sweat on her forehead.

"My little JJ bird." Jon's voice broke the silence.

JJ snapped around, and her eyes widened with recognition. Jon leaned against a tree twenty feet from her, wearing a smug smile and holding a pistol in one hand that rested on his thigh. A sound suppressor had been screwed onto the end of it.

A dark shade crossed JJ's face. "*Pete.*" The word slithered out of her mouth with disdain.

He chuckled. "I don't go by Pete anymore. Nor do I go by my middle name, Luke."

"Jon? You go by your last name, then?"

"Yep. You and I always went together because of our unique names." His parents were insanely religious and had chosen to name him after Jesus's disciples in the Bible.

"I'm sure your parents didn't know they were naming the devil."

"True." Jon grinned. "But I was their whipping boy—torturing and starving me every time I committed a sin. Who really *is* the devil?"

"Poor boy," she mocked. "Too bad they're not around. You could use more whipping."

The comment wiped the smile from his face and replaced it with a glare.

"What are you doin' here?" JJ asked, perplexed.

"Don't you know? I'm the one they hired to kill you and your daughter. I always told you we'd find our way back to each other. Strange twist of fate, isn't it?"

CHAPTER THIRTY-THREE

Liberty continued to eye Clay warily.

"You don't have to run anymore," Clay assured her.

"Where are the rest of the police? How many are here?"

"It's just me. I told you the truth. I want to bring you in myself. You can trust me."

"Even if I do trust you, I can't trust anyone else." Liberty tightened her grip on the gun. "I know they're going to take my mom away. I'm not ready for that."

"She'll go to a rehab facility. I thought that's what you wanted." He cocked his head sincerely.

"It is. She's sick. She needs help."

"Where is she, Liberty? We need to get you two out of here fast. The man that's after you will not stop until you are both dead. It won't be long before he is here."

She backed up, hesitating. She *wanted* to surrender, wanted to put her full trust in him, but it was her mother. Liberty was afraid of what JJ's reaction would be if Liberty showed up with Clay. It wouldn't be good.

"I need to talk to my mom first. Then I will lead her here. We'll surrender together."

Clay shook his head. "No, I can't let you do that. We need to go together and get her now."

"She's not going to understand. I can't show up with the cops."

"We have to take that chance," Clay pleaded. "We're out of choices. This is for your safety. For *her* safety."

"You don't know my mom. She'll think I betrayed her!" she cried. "She'll think I called you and turned us in."

"We'll work that out later. I'm sorry. I have to take you both now."

He stepped closer, and she withdrew her pistol and pointed it at him with a shaky hand. Clay's eyes widened. "Liberty! What are you doing?"

"I'm sorry. I have to do this." She bit her bottom lip. "You have to let me do it my way."

Clay put his hands up and shook his head and closed his eyes. When he opened them, Liberty saw they were red and wet.

"Your secret life. I see you changing right before my eyes," Clay said. "Why all the secrets and lies?"

"What?" Liberty's face scrunched with his misdirection. "You read my poetry?" Anger heated up inside her.

"You try to hide this secret life from me, but I see it all. You think these drugs will make you happy or take away the pain? They won't. Instead, they will destroy you. They will destroy us."

"What are you doing?" Liberty's tone was stern.

"I found some of your poetry, Liberty. You're very talented. There is truth in them. You know this will destroy both of you. Don't give your mom that power. If you go down that road, she will twist your words. She'll manipulate you and convince you to run."

"That's not going to happen." Liberty shook her head, but her hands holding the gun trembled.

"You know it will, Liberty. Don't fool yourself. You need to trust me. We are out of time. He's going to kill you before you get the chance to surrender. I can't take that chance."

"No," Liberty said, her mind made up. "You have to trust *me*. I am going down to get my mom. You have us, okay? We are not going anywhere. I just need to tell her first."

"How do you think that will go? Honestly?"

"Not well, I'm sure. But I need to try. Go back the way you came. Wait for us. Give me thirty minutes. If I'm not back, then you can come for us. Okay? It's a spot farther down by the lake."

Clay glanced at her gun. "Looks like I don't have a choice."

"Just back away. Slowly," Liberty said. "Back into those trees."

Clay obeyed her demands, walking in reverse until he was in the thicket of trees and she was out of sight.

CLAY KICKED HIMSELF inside. His instincts told him not to let her go. Danger was close.

He approached his car. He decided to call dispatch and disclose his location. Not only was it his duty, but it was the smartest thing to do.

He reached for the handle of the door when a *thuck* sound rang out. Something exploded inside his arm. The bullet from the shooter's gun penetrated his forearm, exited out the back, and ricocheted off his car door, spraying it with spots of blood.

He twisted while reaching for his gun with his left hand. His right hand, his gun hand, was rendered useless. A man marched up the slope toward him, pistol aimed. He had one messed-up eye and the other filled with hate.

Clay withdrew the gun from his holster when the second bullet sang. Clay's head snapped back, and he fell.

CHAPTER THIRTY-FOUR

Liberty's heart raced as she ran back down the trail toward camp. A million thoughts swam through her head. She wondered what she was going to say to her mom to convince her to surrender. She considered telling her the truth. Clay was the one officer they could trust, and he was there to help. They had to give themselves up before the killer showed. She could tell her all of that, but her mother's eyes would narrow, lips would curl in a snarl, and anger would rise. JJ would immediately accuse Liberty of betrayal.

She was not opposed to lying but didn't know which lie would work.

"Mom! The cops are everywhere! They have this whole place surrounded," she could say. "They told me to come and get you. If we walk up the hill to the restrooms, they will take us in without harm."

That story sounded weak. Her mom would see right through it. "Hey, I found a drug dealer up there. He's got heroin!"

That would bring her. Liberty laughed then felt guilty for such a tasteless joke.

Smoke wafted from the camp below, but she couldn't see her mom. JJ could be inside the tent or gathering wood, she supposed. As she neared, her gut warned her that something didn't seem right. Her mother was gone. *Did she bolt?* It was a possibility. Her rational side told her not to jump to conclusions.

She set the pot of water down on the hot coals. She saw the carton of eggs on the rock next to the fire and placed several of them in the pot to boil.

"Mom!" she called out, but only birds chirped. A breeze blew the heavy branches of leaves back and forth. "Mom!" she hollered again and looked inside the tent. It was empty except for a rumpled sleeping bag and saggy pillow.

She walked to the copse of trees behind the camp and saw movement. She caught glimpses of colors from her mother's clothes, and as she cleared more oak trees, she saw JJ. Horror clasped Liberty's throat.

JJ sat on the ground, legs stretched out in front of her and back against a tree. Her arms were splayed on her thighs, palms up, and her head hung between her legs. Liberty saw ribbons of gray, and it quickly registered as duct tape. JJ's entire midsection was wrapped in it, strapping her to the tree. But that wasn't all. JJ's arms were wrapped in duct tape down to the elbow, and there was something odd about her arms. Things were attached, syringes fastened to her arms with the same tape. One needle was inserted in each arm, and they were filled with a dark-yellow liquid.

"Mom?" Liberty's trembling voice cried.

JJ lifted her heavy head of long hair as if dipped in molasses. She raised her bloodshot eyes, and tears streaked her face.

"Lib... er... ty." Her words dragged. "*Run.*"

"Mom? What happened?" She ignored the warning and crept closer.

"Run, baby... *run.*"

"Where is he?" Liberty placed her hand on the gun hilt and looked left to right but couldn't see anyone. "I gotta get you out of this."

"Honey, you gotta go," JJ begged.

Liberty ignored her mother's pleas and eyed the syringes. They were going to be tricky to remove. She needed something sharp. "I gotta get a knife. I'll be right back."

She turned to run back to the camp and froze. A man dressed in a dark-gray T-shirt, black pants, and cowboy boots stood in her way. He held a gun down at his side and stood with a crooked lean that rang a bell. Pete used to stand that way.

A flash of memories of Pete, leaning in the archway to the kitchen with one leg straight and a slight bend in the other, flooded her head.

The man before her was no doubt Pete, the despicable creature who had beaten and tortured her mom years ago. Her eyes darted between the trees. Pete was the only other soul around. *Is he the killer? Could that be possible?*

"Hey, Libby. Long time, no see." Pete smirked.

Liberty hated it when Pete called her that. She reached behind her and gripped the gun but froze when he lifted his pistol and aimed it at her.

"No, no," he warned. "Don't do that. I'd hate to cover your mother with your splattered brains. Wouldn't be pleasant." He shook his head.

Keeping his gun aimed at her, Pete approached. "Turn around, girl. Slowly, and let's see your hands."

She obeyed, and Liberty felt Pete withdraw the pistol from the back of her pants. It sounded like he stuffed it into the back of his own. Then he kicked her rear end and sent her sprawling. She hit the dirt in a cloud of dust, and rocks pressed into her. Pete laughed as if her fall was funny.

"Knock it off, Pete!" JJ roared. "Leave her outta this. I'm the one who killed Billy Ray. Let her go, an' you can kill *me.*"

"You didn't kill that boy any more than Liberty did. Any fool can see that. You don't have it in you to kill a guy like that." He grinned.

"*Why not?* I nearly killed you."

Pete touched the scar on his forehead and his damaged, sunken eye as if remembering, and his smirk disappeared. "That was a good hit with the bat, I'll give you that, but it didn't come close to killing me."

With the muzzle of his gun, he motioned for Liberty to move closer, and she shuffled her body next to JJ's. *Clay was right.* She regretted not trusting him, but she couldn't think of that then. *Where is he?*

The officer was the one hope she had. If they could stall Pete for long enough, Clay could surprise him and take him out.

"I made a mistake," Pete said. "Two things wrong with that Christmas night years ago. First, I got drunk. I don't let alcohol manipulate me anymore. Second, I lost control. That's when mistakes happen."

"Is that supposed to be an apology?" JJ asked.

"No. I don't apologize. You both needed a beating that night. Your little bitch of a daughter never listened to the rules. So, no, I'm not sorry. I'd just be more controlled about it now. More methodical. Back then, they said I was *damaged* by my tours in Iraq and Afghanistan. The things I'd witnessed. Or maybe it was because of my own abusive parents. A lot of shit happened to me in my life. Until I met the man who got me into this business. He taught me everything. Taught me how to control my behavior and my anger. To stop letting things *happen* to me. I learned to hone my rage and funnel it into something more productive. Instead of being a victim, I am now the one that makes things happen to other people." He beamed.

Pete stepped closer and crouched to their eye level. "I am Legion. I am the devil. I'm the one people fear. People hire me to inflict agony and pain on their victims before I rid this world of them. It's too easy to pull the trigger and off someone fast and move on. It takes precision and talent to do what I do. Some call it torture. I call it karma. You two hurt me back then. Especially you." He shook a finger at JJ. "I have been a patient man. I wanted to track you down, find you, and smash in your skull. Ohhh, so *bad* I wanted to. But good things come to those who wait. I had faith that my day would come, and when it did, it would be the right moment. Life has a way of doing that, and you must master the art of tolerance to ride it out. So you can imagine my surprise when I got the call, and my next target was you! *Wooo!*" he wailed. "Karma! Life rewarded me, and I've waited so long."

"You are right." Liberty flared, and Pete turned to her. "Karma did come back around but not to reward you. It's to reward me." She gritted her teeth. "I've waited a long time to see your face again. I had to wait until I was old enough and strong enough to pick up a rock and smash your face in. You've got it all wrong, *Pete*!" she hissed. "Karma brought you to *us*."

Pete laughed, and JJ looked at her daughter with surprise.

"You're old enough now, huh? Strong?" He waved her off with a dismissive hand.

"You beat my mom. No, you nearly pummeled her to death. It took months for her to recover. Physically, anyway. Mentally, I'm still not sure. Now she's hooked on heroin because of *you*. You son of a bitch!"

Pete laughed. "I love family reunions."

"You're *not* family!" Liberty glared. "You never were. You are just a weak little man. Nothing more."

"Weak?" His smile disappeared. "Look who's in control."

"You are so insecure, it's pitiful. You always have been. That's why you fight for control and beat poor, defenseless women and six-year-old girls. Wow. That takes a real strong man." Liberty squinted her eyes while nodding.

Pete's face burned red.

"You had to have so many rules," Liberty continued. "You had to have that stupid, silly list of yours. What were those rules for? *Huh?* Can you tell me?" Liberty held her place. Her body stopped shaking from fear. Her eyes never wavered as she glared at Pete. "Just so you could have control over us? You are so helpless. You're actually just ruling the things and people around you so you can hide your real weaknesses. And the truth is, you are pathetic. You talk about controlling your anger and finding these new ways of living life—*no*. It's just new ways to hide the fact that nobody loves you. And you can't love anyone because you don't love yourself."

JJ's gaze lowered, and a corner of her mouth lifted into a smile as she looked at her daughter again. Liberty was confident and strong, and it'd felt good to say those words. She'd emptied her soul of much of the anger she harbored for Pete, and she felt herself letting go of the fear of him that had always haunted her.

Then she saw the rage build in Pete, and it was about to explode. *Is that a good thing?* He expressed earlier how it was one of his weaknesses, yet it could turn ugly quick. They were not in any position of defense.

Pete burned his dark eyes into Liberty, and his words deepened to a demonic growl. "You little *shit*! You wouldn't talk to me that way if I was still your daddy."

He struck like a viper with a backhand across Liberty's face. The blow nearly knocked her over, but she bounced back, her cheek burning. Pete jumped on her and forced her to the ground. He covered her mouth with one hand, and the other hand pressed the barrel of the gun to her temple. His knee was pressed into her gut.

"I should blow your brains out right now." Pete stared into her eyes. His one good eye darted back and forth across her, as if deliberating. Liberty tried to reach her arms around his back to find the pistol in his pants, but her awkward position didn't allow for it.

"But that's not the plan," he finished. He stood up and pulled Liberty to her feet by her hair, twisted her, then shoved her down in front of her mother.

"If you're thinking your officer friend is coming to save you, I hate to disappoint, but I already killed him. Bullet to the head. Right between the eyes."

An icy claw caught the breath in her throat, and she turned to him with a frightened, puzzled look.

He nodded. "Right after you left him. Back up there by the restrooms." He hooked a thumb behind him. "I followed you down the hill when I was done."

Liberty was ready to burst into a mix of tears and rage. Shock, terror, and grief overtook her, but she quickly sucked the emotions back in and buried them for later. She couldn't feel them right then. She had to survive.

Pete took in deep breaths as if attempting to cool his rage. "We still have a game to play." He smirked.

CHAPTER THIRTY-FIVE

While on her hands and knees, facing her mom, Liberty searched the ground for something, anything that could be a weapon or cut her mom's ties. There were leaves, twigs, and a large dead branch. She saw a flat rock with a sharp edge. If she could grab it, she might be able to saw through the tape, but Pete was keeping his eyes and gun on them.

"All right, you two. The time has come. And it's quite simple. I'm letting you both off too easy with this one, so I just need you to do what I say. In front of you is your mom. Dear, sweet Mom. The one who raised you around her drug habit. There are two syringes. One in each arm. I carefully poked each needle into a vein. I'm sure they're swelling up now and burning. I filled one syringe with heroin. A simple dose. One that JJ, in her state, can clearly handle. One that will give her that instant warm, comforting feeling. You feel it rush through your body like a smooth stream."

JJ closed her eyes. It looked to Liberty as if she was fighting the temptation. Like the heroin was calling to her. Beyond the immediate terror they faced, that damned heroin wouldn't *shut up*.

"In the other syringe is heroin with a little something else. Fentanyl. Enough to overdose her body and kill her. I'm surprised to see she hasn't shot up either one yet. I taped up her body in such a way that if she really wanted to, she could have done it herself."

Liberty looked at her mother's hands and the syringes. The tape came down to her elbows. Pete was right. JJ could have injected the heroin. Lord knew she needed it. But when she looked into her mother's eyes, she saw something different there. Something she hadn't seen in a long, long time. Strength.

"I couldn't, Lib. I won't. I won't," JJ managed between sobs.

"The decision is yours, Liberty. Which will it be?" Pete asked.

Liberty turned and glowered at Pete. That was the cruelest thing he could have done to them. Either Liberty shot her mom up with the drug that fueled her addiction—the cause of so much pain and suffering in their lives—or she shot her mom up with the fluid of death. Either way, Liberty was killing her. One meant instant death, and the other one was slow.

"And what happens next? What if I choose the right one? If I choose the heroin and all she gets is high, then what?" Liberty asked.

He shrugged smugly. "I'll let you go."

"No, you won't. You were hired to kill us."

"Well, we'll just have to see about that, won't we?"

There was no seeing about it. Liberty knew it was their end. Pete would not stop until they were both dead.

She turned back to her mom. If she chose the right one, perhaps she'd have a chance. It might give her an opportunity to fight back. She glanced between the fluids, which looked similar. The one on the right was a shade darker, but she didn't know what that meant.

"Which one is it?" she asked her mom.

"Don't." Her mother shook her head. "I will do it."

"Just tell me. Which one's the heroin?" Liberty asked.

JJ looked at both.

"Can you tell? Which one looks right?"

JJ glanced to each one again. She turned her sorrowful eyes to Liberty. "I don't know."

CHAPTER THIRTY-SIX

Clay's head and arm were on fire. As he wiped the wetness from his lips and opened his eyes, his vision blurred. His back hurt from rocks and roots in the ground, and he rolled to his side. Blood and broken shards of glass surrounded him like crumbs. He placed a palm to his head, and it came away red with blood. He cradled his wounded, bleeding arm.

Clay remembered the flash of the gun. He'd felt the thud against his forehead and had fallen back. That was the last he could recall.

But if the bullet hit my head, how am I still alive? It baffled him. He studied his car. There was a bullet hole in the door, surrounded by spots of blood. That was the first shot that had gone through his arm. It had passed in and out. The driver's-side window was completely shattered. That had been the second bullet. *Did that go in and out too?*

He was no doctor, but he was sure he wouldn't be alive if that had been the case. It wasn't possible. He struggled to his feet, still holding on to his arm. He had to stop the bleeding. He took his shirt off then the T-shirt beneath and wrapped them around the wound. He tied it off tight, using his teeth, then cradled his arm again. Blood still trickled from the wound in his forehead but wasn't leaking like he thought it should be.

He leaned against his car, looked at the shattered window again, then scanned the ground around him and the pieces of glass. There was blood on the pavement but mostly from his arm, not his head. That puzzled him even more.

He questioned how the bullet had exited his head then had struck the window. *Easy,* he told himself. *You were standing right in front of it when you were hit. It went straight into your head, out the back, and into the glass.*

But he'd been standing next to his car and window, not in front of it. It still didn't make sense. He stood taller than the vehicle. The angle hadn't been right for the bullet to go through his head then shatter his window.

He winced as he probed the wound in his head. It was one-eighth of an inch deep, but that was it. Just a flesh wound that stung like hell. He retraced the events. He'd twisted at the first gunshot, reaching with his left hand for his gun when the second shot had rung out.

He'd stepped back. He *remembered* stepping back.

Clay looked at the ground where he'd been standing. A thick root from a nearby tree protruded from the dirt and had caused him to trip. The pieces finally came together.

He'd tripped while stepping back as the bullet simultaneously raced for his head. He must have twisted his face at the same time in response to protect his fall. Because of that, the bullet's target had been off. Instead, it had grazed his head and had ricocheted when a minute portion of the bullet had touched his skull. It had been enough to change its trajectory to smash into the window.

It had been nothing short of a miracle. Someone or something from above was watching out for him. Many people could discern that as a simple coincidence. *Perhaps.* But even if that was so, it had worked so perfectly that the shooter had been tricked into thinking Clay had been shot in the head and had died. His wife was looking out for him. It was his Sam. He had no doubt.

Clay was thankful that the killer hadn't slowed down and taken the time to notice there had not been a splatter of brains, bone, and blood out the back of his head.

Liberty! His heart leaped. The killer was there. Liberty and her mother were in immediate danger. He had to find them quickly. He wiped the blood from his forehead, grasped his gun with his left hand, then charged down the path he'd seen Liberty descend. He only hoped he was not too late.

CHAPTER THIRTY-SEVEN

Liberty stared at the syringes, unable to perform Pete's directive. She racked her brain for escape ideas, but nothing came to her.

"Time is up," Pete said. "Push one of them in, Libby."

"Don't call me that."

"You're hardly in the right position for demands."

"What happens if I choose not to?"

"Like Dirty Harry says, you've made my day. I'll pull you aside, and with my knife, I'll filet you in front of your mother. And I'll keep you alive while I do it."

Liberty rested her hand on the left syringe, debating. She looked at the ground to her right, at the rock with the jagged edge. *Could I grab it and start cutting mom's bonds or at least hand it to her without him seeing?* She pushed her right leg out to use her body to block more of his line of sight and reached for the rock.

Thump! Pete fired a shot that hit the dirt just above her hand. It hit the rock, and splinters flew.

"Don't even think of it, honey. I am out of patience. You have ten seconds to pick a syringe. Matter of fact... you only need one hand to do it. Place your right hand on the ground. Stretch it out."

Liberty slowly stuck her hand out, held back a whimper, and closed her eyes.

"Oh, shut the hell up, Petey!" JJ hollered. "If you're going to kill us, then do it!"

"What's that, J-Bird?" His dark eye went wild.

"Quit playing your games! Have you really got the balls or not? 'Cause neither me nor my daughter are gonna do it. We ain't gettin' outta this alive, so we are gonna go out *our* way."

"Finally, the mother bitch chimes in!" Pete said.

"Put your hand back, honey," JJ said softly.

Liberty sat back. Then she noticed something.

When Pete had shot the rock, it had broken into three pieces. One of them had landed next to JJ's thigh. JJ seemed to be keeping his attention by talking as she turned the rock up in her fingers and slowly sawed at her bonds. Pushing his buttons had worked for Liberty earlier, and apparently, JJ was going to use the same tactic.

"I'll bet you're not even supposed to kill us. They hired you to bring us to them. That's why we're not dead."

Pete stayed silent. Thoughts appeared to swim behind his eye. JJ was getting under his skin.

"That's it, isn't it? You're *not* supposed to kill us. You need to bring us in to them. *Ha!* You're not in control after all. All this bullshit about 'I'm in control of myself—'"

"Shut *up!*" he yelled, cutting her off. "*Fucking bitches!*" He ran over and pushed Liberty out of his way. She toppled and rolled. He depressed the syringe in JJ's left arm.

Liberty snatched up a rock, twisted around, and brought it down on Pete's head. He shook his head once, but it didn't seem to faze him. Pete snapped a blow to the side of her skull with the butt of his pistol, and the lights went out for Liberty.

CLAY FOLLOWED THE TRAIL to JJ's camp quickly and cautiously. He slowed as he neared, keeping discreetly behind bushes and trees. From his distance, he could see the camp, but it looked empty.

Where are they?

He trotted to the firepit. The pot of water boiled over and splashed on the hot coals, and the cracked eggs bobbed up and down. He pushed the pot from the fire with a log. Silence surrounded him, and he worried.

The tall trees knew the secret of what had happened but refused to speak. They stood like sentries, swaying in the wind. Birds chirped, and he heard the tide of the lake lap against the shore. He edged into the grove near the camp and saw remnants of duct tape hanging from a tree. More stips of it were on the ground. Someone must've been tied up. Upon closer inspection, he found drops of blood and two syringes. One of them was full of yellow liquid, and the other was empty.

His shoulders sank in despair. They were gone. The killer had taken them.

CHAPTER THIRTY-EIGHT

Liberty awoke with a screaming headache. Immense pain pounded inside her head as if it wanted to escape. Her vision blurred as she opened her eyes to darkness. The surface she lay on was hard, and her body ached. She tried to bring her hands to her throbbing head, but they wouldn't move. They were bound behind her back. She felt the bulk of a body pressed up against her front, and her butt touched something hard like metal. She was sandwiched in darkness.

A constant rushing sound like a powerful wind whipped against the walls that surrounded her. She couldn't quite make it out. She lifted her body to sit up, but a metal roof stopped her short.

She pressed her eyes in the darkness to make out her surroundings. As she twisted in her tight space, she found a crack in the floor beneath her. It was a rusted spot in the metal, and she got a glimpse of the outside world. Black pavement moved at a high rate of speed below. She was inside the trunk of a car. The rushing sound was the traffic on the road, and she heard the rattling of the running engine. She assumed the other body was her mother.

"Mom?"

No answer. She rolled into JJ and kneed her back.

"Mom?"

JJ groaned and moved.

"Mom, are you okay?"

"L-L-L-Liberty?" she groaned. "Where are we?"

The car hit a bump. Their bodies popped up then slammed back down on the hard metal, and they both groaned in pain.

"We're in a car. He took us. We have to get out of here," Liberty said.

Liberty looked around. Her eyes were still swimming from the blow from Pete's gun, but she quickly regained focus to see clearly. She struggled to roll around to face the rear of the vehicle, bumping into her mom several times and banging her shoulders and knees, but was unable to. She saw a bit of light through the trunk's keyhole but not enough to illuminate anything.

Liberty stretched her neck to find the plastic lever that released the trunk from inside. After several minutes of feeling around, she realized that either the car was too old to have one, or it had been cut off. She gasped in defeat.

Her mother moaned and mumbled incoherently. Liberty's last memory was of Pete pushing one of the syringes, filling her mom with either heroin or death. JJ panted, and she groaned. But she was still alive. If Pete had injected her with the overdose, her mother wouldn't still be there. It was more likely that he didn't plan to overdose her at all. *Otherwise, why would he take both of us somewhere else?*

Liberty pushed against the back seat of the car, trying to break through. After five hard hits with her elbow and fists, the seat moved slightly, and she saw a crack of light at the top.

Then a sharp voice cried out from the front. "Knock it off!"

A shot rang out, and the bullet pierced the back seat and exited out the trunk next to Liberty. Trembling, she felt a sudden urge to pee. *That was close!*

"I'll fill that trunk full of bullets!" Pete's muffled voice hollered.

Liberty sank, defeated.

CHAPTER THIRTY-NINE

Clay sped down the freeway toward Tulsa. He'd searched the entire area for JJ and Liberty and had found nothing. He spoke to Calloway through his car's Bluetooth speakers.

"There's a Ford Escape parked back near the campsite," Clay exclaimed. "And further down, there's a black Dodge Ram off the side of the road. It could be the black truck that the couple at the motel saw, but no sign of JJ's car. The Escape belongs to her sister. Apparently, Liberty snuck out of their house and took off in it. I spoke to Serene, and she told me JJ is driving a beat-up Oldsmobile Cutlass Supreme from the seventies. Since I don't see the Oldsmobile, they must have left in that."

"Not a good choice," Calloway said.

"I think the killer took them in the Oldsmobile because it's disposable. I need a team at Lake McMurtry to investigate the grounds and run the plates on the Dodge. I need to know everything."

"What do you think he's trying to do?" Calloway asked.

"He's taking them somewhere else to finish the job. He didn't want to kill them there. I don't know why or where he'd take them, and I'm running out of time. Have you had any luck tracking the GPS location on her phone?"

"No. I tried it again a few minutes ago and got nothing," Calloway said.

Inside, Clay was kicking himself. He *never* should have walked away from Liberty. He should have talked to her more, and he should have *never* let her go. *But she had a gun on you.* She wouldn't have shot him.

He was sure of it. He'd had his one chance to save her, and he'd blown it.

"Where are you heading now?" Calloway asked.

"For Tulsa. That's where Rick Pines lives. The only thing I can guess is he's bringing them to Rick."

"You might be onto something. We just got a call from an RN that works at Stillwater Medical Center. He was there when Rick's family showed up to identify Billy Ray. He says he overheard Rick's mother order Jemma and her daughter to be killed. The RN passed it off at first, thinking it was just a distraught mother spouting out anger, but the more he thought of it, the more the conversation bothered him. He said, 'It was the way she said it. So cold and determined.'"

"His mother?" Clay asked.

"Yes."

"That's it then. He is bringing them to Tulsa so the family can kill them personally."

"Could be," Calloway said.

"Can you text me the address to his home, his mother's home, and his place of business?"

"Yeah, no problem. And Hank is putting a team together right now to rendezvous with you."

"Perfect. Thanks." He ended the call then rang Liberty's phone again. It went to voice mail.

CHAPTER FORTY

Curled up on the hard floor of the trunk, feeling every bump and turn, Liberty sobbed. She'd searched as best as she could for her phone or her mom's but was positive Pete had taken them. He would have been stupid not to. She also searched for a weapon or tool to cut their bonds but found nothing.

Are you okay? Her conscience spoke again, soothing her.

No.

She thought of the officer, Clay, the poor guy who'd desperately tried to help them. *Is he really dead?* And for Pete to be the killer. *He used to live with us!* The cruelty and irony of it all was too surreal to process.

Liberty cried for her mother, who lay next to her. JJ's body was still convulsing and was slick with sweat, and she'd thrown up twice in the trunk. The odor was rancid and sour. Liberty continued to talk to her mom, but JJ's only responses were mumbles and groans. Her mom was sick and getting worse. Perhaps there had been something in the injection that'd made her sick.

"Keep fighting, Mom."

Liberty scooted her body next to JJ and leaned her forehead against her mom's frail back. She felt the heat and quick beats of JJ's heart. Her mother's vulnerability and sickness flooded the trunk. Liberty wept into the back of her shirt.

Memories surfaced. It was Liberty's tenth birthday, and her mom had wanted to make it special. She took Liberty to dinner at Martha's Diner, a local favorite, and JJ's current employer. She had worked as a waitress there for a few years, and Liberty had spent many afternoons

190

after school in the corner booth doing homework and waiting for her mom to clock out. Charly, the owner and chef, was a large, jovial man who always carried a smile and a warm spirit. Charly had treated Liberty with ice cream and grilled cheese sandwiches many times. There were two other waitresses, Kelly and Dawn, who were like second moms to Liberty. For the three years JJ had worked at Martha's, Liberty had a family, and that was no exception on her tenth birthday.

She had the entire menu to order from, and Liberty was drawn to breakfast. She ordered pancakes, eggs, bacon, sausage, hash browns, a slice of ham and toast, and chocolate milk. Her mom ordered coffee.

"Aren't you getting anything?" Liberty asked.

"No, I'm not hungry." She waved a hand.

Liberty scrunched her face, unbelieving.

"I ate earlier." JJ shrugged.

"Well, I got a lot of food. You can help me eat it."

"Got it. Before your smorgasbord gets here, birthday girl, open your presents."

JJ handed her two gift bags and a card. She read the card first—it was etiquette—and her mom had written a ton of meaningful words. She'd expressed her love. Liberty teared up and fanned her face with the card.

"I'll reread that later 'cause I'll cry all over the place." Liberty chuckled.

JJ glowed with excitement as Liberty tore through the gifts. A cute blouse, a tank top, socks, and a gift card to her favorite music store. It was like Christmas.

"Mom, I can't believe it."

"Like it?"

"I love it. These are so cute. And then a gift card? It's so much. You shouldn't have."

"You deserve it."

When the food came, Liberty dug in and scooted the plate closer to her mom to share. JJ picked at a few things with her fork.

After dinner, Charly, Kelly, and Dawn came out with a small cake with a large lit candle in the center. They all sang "Happy Birthday" to her and told her that they loved her. Liberty had been elated. It was one of her favorite moments, and as she looked back, she could read the underlying truth. Her mom hadn't had enough money to feed them both. She'd spent all she had to get her daughter gifts and a special birthday dinner.

It was sad that, a few months later, JJ had been caught stealing then had been fired from that job. Liberty was sure that Charly and her coworkers were aware of JJ's drug habit. They'd have had to be blind not to. And like that, Liberty lost her surrogate family.

Liberty still held resentment toward her mom. Time after time, JJ's drug habit had pushed everyone away and had driven them down a path of poverty, depression, and danger. But then, as she watched her mother breathing heavily next to her in the trunk, fighting for her life, she couldn't help but remember the good times. Her mother was still *in* there. Liberty knew it and still carried hope.

"Oh, Mom. Please hang on. I need you," she pleaded. "Dear Lord, if you're listening. My mom needs your help. *Real bad.* I know we haven't been the best and haven't made the right choices, but my mom is a good person. She's... she's a good mom!" she cried. She hadn't been able to say that for many years. "She's my mom, and I *need* her." She took a deep breath and calmed herself. "For a woman who's been dealt a lot of bad cards in her life, she's done her best, and she deserves some help. *Please* help her. Help *me*. Amen."

She kept her eyes closed and head against JJ until her tears dried up. She pulled away, shuffled back, and pressed her head to the floor. She turned her eyes to the small rust opening below and watched the asphalt race past. It was a small view into freedom. How she longed to be on the outside, away from the sweltering, claustrophobic trunk. Her window was a sharp, rusted hole, and a thought crept in.

It was *jagged* and sharp.

It had been staring her in the face that whole time. She quickly rolled to her back and carefully slid along the floor until she felt the hole with her fingers. The edge cut her flesh. She lowered her hands a bit until her duct tape bonds were over its jagged ridges. She moved her hands up down and pressed hard until she felt the bonds tear and heard them rip. Excitement boomed.

The car braked suddenly. Liberty and JJ rolled and banged their heads. Liberty feared that Pete somehow knew she was trying to free herself.

She listened. All she heard was the idling of the engine. After a minute, the car resumed as if they'd only been stopped at a light.

He must be off the freeway and into the city. Which city that was, she didn't know, but it probably meant they were closer to their destination.

She shifted back into position. Her mom had rolled onto the hole, so Liberty pushed her off. Liberty quickly situated herself again and commenced cutting. The edge was small, so it was a slow process.

CHAPTER FORTY-ONE

Clay had three addresses texted to him. One was for Rick's business, Pines Pest Control. It was a front, Clay suspected, used to launder money. Another address was for Rick's personal residence, and the third was for his mother's. Hank was already putting together the paperwork to attain search warrants for all three. Because of limited time, Clay didn't have the luxury of waiting for Hank's team to start checking. He had to start with one. It was like choosing to check Boomer Lake or Lake McMurtry. It could make all the difference.

Would he take them to his business? True, it worked as a cover for his real business, but since it was in the public eye, Clay figured the killer wouldn't take them there. He headed straight for Rick's home, a large, modern house on the outskirts of town. Clay parked his car two houses away and walked the rest of the distance.

The house consisted of numerous large windows, and many of them didn't have blinds. A bay window provided a view into the living room, which was empty and unlit. The house looked deserted. No cars in the driveway or curbside. No sign of life.

He knocked on the door and rang the bell several times before concluding it wasn't the place. To make sure, he snuck into the backyard, where he stirred up a sleeping pit bull. The dog leaped to his feet and charged him, barking ferociously. Clay barely made it to the gate and slammed it shut inches before the animal caught up.

Assured he could check that address off his list, he jumped into his car and sped for Rick's mother's house. He called Hank, whose team was still twenty minutes out, and told him the update.

"That's one place down," Hank said. "If you get there first, wait for us. These are dangerous men."

"Of course," Clay said.

"I mean it. No hero stuff. He'll have a small army around him."

"Got it," Clay said, knowing he couldn't keep the promise. Liberty's and her mom's lives were in danger, and he blamed himself for not grabbing them when he'd had the chance. He wasn't about to let them die while waiting for Hank.

CHAPTER FORTY-TWO

With her body drenched in sweat, her clothes pasted to her skin, and her long hair plastered against her scalp, Liberty couldn't last much longer in the oven the trunk had become. Tiny bits of air seeped in but not nearly enough. The metal around them cooked from the hot sun and burned at the touch.

She'd finally succeeded in cutting her bonds, though, and worked on her mom's.

"Lib... er... ty?" JJ moaned.

"Mom? How are you doing? Are you okay?"

"Feel sick," JJ said. "Heavy like concrete. Mouth dry."

"I know. Hang in there, Mom. I'm trying to get your ties cut. Can you roll a little more to the left? I can't quite reach your wrists."

JJ rolled, and Liberty attacked the bonds with her fingers, but they held strong. She couldn't bust them without a tool.

"Water?" JJ cried.

"Sorry. I don't have any. Hopefully soon."

"Where are we?"

"I think we're in the trunk of the Oldsmobile. He tied us up and put us in here. He's taking us somewhere."

Liberty shuffled through the trunk again in search of anything she could use to cut her tape. She found a hot, dusty blanket that kicked up particles in the air and triggered a coughing fit. She pushed it out of their way. There was nothing else.

"Here." Liberty pulled her mom to her, attempting to position her onto the rusted hole.

The car stopped abruptly, and they rolled again.

"Shit." Liberty hurried to reposition her mom.

The car door squeaked open, and she heard footsteps.

Liberty started to move her mom's wrists up and down. The jagged edge started to cut through the bonds but not enough. She heard the key enter the lock of the trunk. Liberty thrust her hands behind her back so as not to alert the killer that she'd freed herself. Although the duct tape had been cut enough to separate her wrists, the tape was still attached to her skin. So she hoped as long as she kept her wrists together, her bonds would appear unbroken. The moment to escape was not then. She had to stay patient, wait it out, and find the right time.

The trunk creaked open, and sunlight blinded them except for the space occupied by the tall dark figure.

"Still alive in there?" Pete poked at them.

"Barely," Liberty muttered.

"I just realized I didn't give either of you water during that long trip. So sorry." He opened a water bottle and poured it on them. He laughed as it splashed down each of their faces.

"Come on, little pumpkins." Pete grabbed Liberty's arm and butt, hoisted her out of the trunk, and let her fall to the ground. Liberty's instincts wanted to bring her hands around to protect her fall, but she knew it would ruin any chance she had. She twisted to land shoulder first, hit the ground, and rolled as Pete dropped JJ beside her.

Pete pulled bandanas from his back pocket. "Gotta blindfold ya now."

"What is the purpose of that if you're going to kill us?" Liberty asked.

"I know." He chuckled. "Not sure, but my employer is a stickler for it. He's real cautious."

He blindfolded each of them then walked them into what Liberty believed was a house. They moved through it and were guided to turn two times. Liberty banged her shoulder into a wall, and the pain was intense. Pete shoved her forward, and she tumbled to the hardwood floor.

Her instincts were to thrust her arms out to catch her fall, and her left arm did slightly, but fearing that Pete would notice her cut bonds, she quickly pulled it back. She hit the ground with her shoulder and rolled onto her back. Then she heard what must have been her mother rolling next to her. A door slammed shut, and Liberty heard a lock turn. Silence surrounded them again. The floorboards echoed with each footstep. It wasn't as hot as the trunk, but the air was stagnant, and dust swirled about them.

JJ groaned in pain. "Where are we?"

"I don't know. In someone's house, I think."

Liberty needed more water. The saliva had almost evaporated completely from her mouth. It might as well have been filled with hot sand.

Footsteps and voices from beyond their room reached Liberty's ears, and the sounds got louder until their door was thrown open.

"Whoaaa! You got 'em, all right! Mom, did I tell you this guy is good or what?" a man's voice spoke.

"You done good, son," a woman's voice, low and keen, said.

Footsteps approached Liberty, and her blindfold was pulled off. Her vision was blurry at first, but once she refocused, she stared up at an old woman. Her gray hair was tied back in a tight bun, mouth taut and outlined by frown wrinkles, and her eyes were an ice-blue fire that blazed.

Liberty's eyes darted away from the woman's glare. They were in a small and empty bedroom lined with wood paneling. It appeared to have not been used in years.

JJ had slid down to the floor, and Pete sat her back up. The lady pulled the blindfold from JJ, who kept her head down. "You two took my son away."

"No," Liberty cut in. "We didn't kill him. He came—"

"Shut up!" The old woman struck Liberty across the cheek with her bare hand. "I'll bust yer teeth right out, bitch!"

Liberty tasted blood in her mouth and swallowed.

"Leave... her *alone*," JJ managed in her sick state. That time, Pete smacked her. JJ's eyes rolled into the back of her head, and she looked like she was close to passing out.

"You are a vile, wretched, worthless piece a' shit! Both a' ya!" the old woman hollered and spat into each of their faces.

Liberty tried to shove the thought of saliva dripping down her cheek away. *Put it on the shelf, and deal with it later.*

"It is time for a reckonin'. We will have justice."

"That's their name." The unknown man smirked.

The old woman turned her head slowly, burning her stare into him.

"*Justice.* It's their last name. Ironic, that's all," he said apologetically.

"I know, Rick. Do I look stupid to you?"

"No, Ma. Sorry."

Rick's mother turned back to JJ and Liberty. "Get this filth ready for the firin' range."

The old woman left them and walked out of the room. Rick and Pete remained. Pete stayed close to the front door with his arms crossed. Rick eyed Pete.

"I should have killed them at the campsite." Pete scowled.

"These bitches killed *my* brother. The kill is rightfully ours."

"*You* should have hunted them, then."

"That's what we hired you for." Rick leered and approached JJ. "Why did you kill my brother?"

It took a moment for JJ to raise her head and look up at him. Her eyelids were half-open. "I didn't. He came to my house to kill me. Tried to kill my daughter too."

"You stole *him* from *me*! When you and your boyfriend beat the shit out of Billy Ray and took his cash, who do you think that belonged to?"

"I... I don't know what you're talkin' 'bout."

"It's true!" Liberty jumped in. "It's just my mom and me. She didn't hurt anybody, and she didn't steal your money." Liberty glanced at her mom with sadness. JJ's body wavered left to right, threatening to collapse. "She is sick. With whatever that asshole shot her up with." Liberty jerked her head in Pete's direction. "We need water, and she needs an ambulance. Murdering us won't give you peace because you're killing the wrong people."

"Are you saying Billy Ray died in someone else's house?" Rick sneered. "'Cause he was found in *your* home. Did the boogeyman do it? Did your boyfriend?"

"Mom's boyfriend was long gone by the time your brother showed up. Someone else beat him up. I promise you, my mom has no money." She shook her head, exhausted.

Rick turned to Pete, who shrugged. "I found no money on them or at their house. The boyfriend had it all. You should have received the package."

"We did," Rick said.

Liberty tilted her head. *Received the package?* She wanted to ask him what that meant but didn't get the chance.

JJ's eyes rolled to the back of her head, and drool dripped from her mouth as her head tipped back against the wall. She seemed to be fading again.

"Is she gonna make it?" Rick asked Pete. "What did you give her?"

"Just a dose of heroin and a little extra. Nothing she can't handle. She'll be fine."

Rick gawked at him. "She'd better be. If she dies first, Momma's gonna wanna replace you as target practice."

"Be my guest." Pete stared into Rick's eyes, unflinching.

CHAPTER FORTY-THREE

Hank's team arrived at Judith Pines's house at the same time as Clay. A SWAT team of five men plus Hank and Clay approached the house stealthily and spread out. With practiced precision, they covered each exit of the house, the sides, back, and front. All of them were dressed in protective gear and were equipped with AR15 and MP5 automatic rifles. Clay and Hank strapped bulletproof vests over their shirts, and Hank carried a shotgun while Clay armed himself with his nine-millimeter pistol.

Clay crept around a copse of trees and followed Hank and the SWAT captain to the front door. The simple ranch-style home sat quiet and unaware. There was one vehicle in the driveway but no sign of the Oldsmobile. If that was the right place, then the vehicle had likely been hidden or discarded elsewhere.

It was all a long shot, and Clay's nerves sparked madness.

Hank had come through in a big way by attaining search warrants and a SWAT team. The narcotics division used them a lot, so Hank knew how to speed one through and which judges to ask.

The SWAT leader, Captain Rice, spoke to his team via earpieces and told them to stand by as he pounded on the door. "Police!" Rice hollered.

Nothing. Rice turned to Clay.

"Let's give it a minute," Clay said.

No sooner did Clay say that when they heard footsteps. They were slow with no urgency in them. Finally, the door cracked open to reveal an older lady in her late seventies. She was short and had a dark complexion, and gray hair hung to her shoulders.

Clay looked to Hank. He wore a doubtful face and shook his head.

"What's this all about?" her meek voice cried.

"Is this the home of Judith Pines?" Clay asked.

"Yes. She's my sister. But she's not home right now."

"We need to inspect your home all the same."

"Do you have a warrant?"

"Yes." Clay withdrew the warrant from his pocket and held it up. The woman studied it then nodded.

"Awright then." She lifted her hands in exasperation and backed away.

CLAY LEANED AGAINST his car next to Hank. They'd made a quick search of the entire house but had found it empty. He bowed his head and ran his hands through his hair in defeat. His face twisted with guilt, and his bloodshot eyes stared off. His wounded arm bled through the bandages he'd wrapped it in, and his injury throbbed.

"You need to get that looked at." Hank nodded to Clay's wound. Clay ignored him.

"What are we doing wrong?" Clay asked.

"Lookin' in the wrong spot."

"I know that."

"There's something we're missing." Hank scrunched his face. "I feel we're on the right track yet not there."

"You know this family better than anyone. You've been working on his case for a long time. Where would they go? What is important to them?" Clay asked.

"They grew up here in Oklahoma. They come from a long line of Pines and hold a lot of pride in their name. They're traditional. Biblical. They take 'an eye for an eye' seriously. It's religion to them. You hurt one member of the family, and you get the whole family down on you. Family feuds. Hatfields-and-McCoys shit." He raised his eyebrows. "You are right, Clay. Our ghost assassin was hired to bring JJ and Liberty in so they can kill those girls themselves. It's how they'd want it. They would not be robbed of that opportunity. All this time, I thought Rick was the head honcho. I'm startin' to think it's his psycho mother. An' they're not stupid. They're not going to kill them where there'd be witnesses or evidence that would link them to the crime. They'd do it where it's safe and remote."

"In the woods?"

"Mmmm, not so sure about that. They'd want to do it somewhere personal but private."

"You mentioned they are from right here in Oklahoma? Where did they grow up?"

Hank's eyes lit up. "Judith's home!"

"That's where we're at," Clay pointed out.

"No. The home *she* grew up in. The one passed down through generations. She'd have inherited it by now."

"Where's that?"

"Let me get to my laptop." He ran to his Chevy Tahoe and jumped in. Clay followed and entered the passenger side.

Hank typed away, paused, typed again, and waited. After a couple of minutes, he smiled and looked at Clay. "Muskogee. She has a house there. It's deep in the woods and sits on twenty acres. It's so old, I'm not sure if it even has electricity or if anyone inhabits it, but it'd be a perfect place to take victims to torture or murder."

CHAPTER FORTY-FOUR

Two of Rick's guards led JJ and Liberty from the empty bedroom down the short hall, through the kitchen, then exited the back door. Liberty was thankful that they weren't blindfolded that time. She eyed their surroundings and hoped to find an advantage for their escape.

They crossed the porch with its wall of stacked firewood and headed for the back of the yard. Liberty clasped her hands together to keep the appearance of being tied up, and she kept her mom between herself and the guards. She didn't want them seeing the back of her at all. JJ seemed to understand that, even in her drugged state, because she would shuffle to the left or right to hide Liberty's hands. Liberty also kept their attention elsewhere by asking a lot of questions.

"Where are we going?" Liberty asked but got no response. "Are they going to kill us? Can we at least get some more water? Last wish kind of thing?"

"Shut up and keep moving," one of the guards said.

On top of a hill was the archery range. Four hay bales stood in a row in front of a line of trees bordering a forest. The bales had paper targets attached, and one of them already held a person.

As Liberty and JJ neared, Liberty saw that the man was tied to the target with rope. His head was slumped over, and long hair draped over his face. The coppery scent of fresh blood surrounded him. Red ran through his hair and dripped onto the dirt below.

The Levi's jacket the man wore looked familiar to Liberty, and JJ's eyes widened as if the sight of him sobered her instantly. She gasped.

The guard yanked JJ and pulled her to the target next to the man. He tied a rope around her body and the bales of hay and tightened the bonds. JJ hung limp. She would probably collapse, if the rope weren't holding her up.

Liberty didn't have much time to consider their escape. Her guard dragged her by the elbow to the next target. She flexed her muscles, held her breath, and expanded her body as much as she could while the man fastened the rope around her. She'd learned from a movie that if she tightened her body while being tied up, she might be able to relax enough to slip out of her bonds easier. No better time than the present to try that out.

Whimpering reached Liberty's ears, and she turned to see her mother crying. Droplets dripped to the dirt. JJ lifted her head to Liberty, blue eyes glistening through her tears. "I'm so sorry."

"It's not your fault," Liberty said, and for the first time, she meant it. Whatever crazy episode had caused this, it wasn't her mom's fault. They were victims of being in the wrong place at the wrong time. Jim Duke had stolen the money from Billy Ray and had left them to pay the price.

JJ turned to the man slumped next to her. He didn't move. Her eyes drooped in sadness.

Across the field, Rick and his mother faced them from forty feet away. Three armed guards spread out behind them. Pete stood far to the right, leaning against a tree. His pistol rested in his hand hanging at his side. He eyed his surroundings like a cautious hunter. Two more guards flanked the sides of the small cabin-like home.

A slight breeze blew past Liberty and cooled the heat and sweat that overwhelmed her body.

Rick approached them and stopped in front of the slumped man next to JJ.

"Look familiar to you?" He smirked at JJ, and she nodded.

He lifted the dead man's head. One of the man's eyes was frozen open in horror, and the other one was swollen shut by bruises. His mouth hung agape, and three arrows pierced his chest, pinning him to the target. His face was mangled from countless blows. Liberty had never seen a more woeful, heartbreaking image. The misery outlined his body and spoke of the pain and torture the poor soul had experienced. It took Liberty longer to recognize him because of his wounds, but it finally struck her. Her mother's boyfriend, Jim Duke, had finally paid his price. Knowing that Jim Duke was the cause of all this nightmare didn't diminish her sense of sympathy for him.

Rick let go of his head, and it fell back in place with a sick sound. "My brother died with a knife thrust through his throat," Rick spoke solemnly. "How long did he sit there coughing and gagging on his blood?"

The images presented themselves to Liberty's mind again with painful intensity.

"And you did *nothin'*!" He pierced JJ with a glare then looked at his mother, who lifted a compound bow with both hands then armed it with an arrow. "You see? We take care of our own. You kill one of us, and we're gonna kill you and yours. That's how it works."

He walked away from them to clear his mother's aim.

JJ's eyes seemed to gain sobriety as she widened them. She pursed her lips, and Liberty saw the fight for life in her. It gave Liberty hope.

The bonds that clasped JJ's hands were slightly cut thanks to Liberty's attempts. JJ continued to wriggle and strain against them but must not have been able to break through. She turned to Pete, who stood nonchalant, watching as the old woman pulled the arrow back and aimed.

JJ looked down the hill at Pete, who stood across the field under the porch. "You gonna let them do this?"

Pete stared with no response.

"If we mean anything to you at all, do something! Isn't there even one thing left in that soul a' yours? Any piece a' decency?"

Thuck! The arrow released. It stuck in the hay inches from JJ's shoulder. Liberty let out a shriek. Liquid spread through her mom's pants at the crotch.

The old woman wore a smug face. "Missed." She smirked, and the rest of them laughed.

JJ gave Liberty a flummoxed look, which she reflected.

JJ turned back to Pete.

"Don't look for sympathy here." Pete shrugged. "They had to beg me to bring you to them. I wanted to end your lives myself. At least I got to play a little game before I did." He gave her a wink.

"You're gonna let them kill your *daughter*?" JJ asked. The words silenced the air and drew dumbfounded looks from both Pete and Liberty.

"Mom?" Both fright and perplexity rang in Liberty's tone.

The old woman eyed Pete then changed the aim of her arrow. Her steel eyes transfixed on Liberty.

Thuck! An arrow landed, slicing Liberty's cheek before it stuck in the hay next to her face. She gasped in momentary relief that the arrow had missed. But the panic quickly returned. *Is it true? Am I his daughter? Why was I never told?* But the sheer terror of another arrow flying kept Liberty's words at bay.

"Hold up, Judith!" Pete called out to the arrow-wielding woman while gesturing with a straight arm and open palm. Judith frowned and set down the arrow in her hand.

Pete crossed the field to JJ and Liberty.

Liberty wrestled with the rope that bound her to the target. She closed her eyes, let out all the air in her lungs, relaxed her muscles, and felt the rope loosen slightly. A small spark of hope and excitement grew. With her free hands, she could push the rope up and over her head and release herself for one shot at escape, but she remained patient and waited for the right moment.

Pete stopped short of Liberty and looked down at her with disdain. He took in her looks with his one good eye. For the first time, she realized they shared the same brown eyes shaped in a downward, sad slant, similar hair color, and even the same nose.

"My daughter, huh?" he grumbled.

"You and I dated for a short while b'fore she was born," JJ said. "Remember? You got deployed, and it wasn't till three years later or so we got back together. She's yours if she's anybody's."

"No. Uh-uh. Can't be." Liberty looked at her mom. "You said my biological father left you before I was born."

"And so he did," JJ said.

"You never said it was this sick *bastard*!"

"No. Why would I?" Tears welled in JJ's eyes. "There was a part of me that knew deep down how evil he was, and I kept that from you to protect you. I was the fool to let him back in. He said he was sorry and that he'd be better. Like an idiot, I believed him. He was good for a while. Until he came after *you*. I knew then he was too dangerous. If I had told him, he'd have been in our lives forever. I couldn't put you through that."

Appearing impatient, Judith turned to Rick, scolding him loud enough for everyone to hear. "What the hell's goin' on? This ain't no family reunion!"

Rick nodded and called to Pete. "Grinder! Let's get on with it!"

Pete held out a hand to them again. "One minute!"

Pete and Liberty stared at each other. Liberty watched as Pete shoved the pistol into the front of his jeans between his gut and belt. He raised his right hand and ran it through her hair. It snagged against the dried sweat, then he ran his fingers down her cheek as she squinted.

"You're my spawn." Pete grimaced. "I missed daddy-daughter days at your school. Missed taking you to summer camp and parent-teacher conferences. I missed teaching you who you should be and how you should act. A' course, you turned out pretty well, considering. You have my strength. I can see that. You've got bite in ya, and you're smart."

Liberty held her rage at bay. Pete's words were buying them time, so she calmed her thoughts and played along.

"Maybe *this* is karma," Liberty said, fighting back the urge to choke on those words and vomit. "Not to have you come back into our lives to kill us. To unite us as a family again."

His eye widened, and tension broke in his face. "Perhaps you're right," Pete said.

Liberty could see his mind spinning and questioning everything he believed about the purpose of karma.

"Jon!" Rick demanded. "Move it, Jon. They're playing you!"

Pete's eye narrowed to a slit, and his face tightened. His pupil shifted to JJ. "You kept her from me all these years? You *lied* to me? You stole thirteen years of a life I could have had with my daughter."

"You didn't want a daughter," JJ said.

"You chose now to tell me?" Pete growled.

"I thought, before we die, you should know."

Rage filled Pete's eye, and his body tightened. "Whore!" He turned to Judith and Rick and pointed at JJ. "You can fire your next shot! Kill this bitch!"

The arrow struck JJ's left shoulder and pinned her arm to the hay. JJ stared at the shaft poking out of her arm in shock and horror before wincing from pain. "Ahhh!"

"*Mom!*"

CHAPTER FORTY-FIVE

It took a painstaking hour for Clay and Hank to find Judith's hide-away cabin in the backwoods near Muskogee, but they wasted no time exiting their vehicles, formulating a plan, then approaching the house.

They heard JJ's scream from behind the house and quickly reformed their group to flank the backyard from both sides. Their professional sniper scaled a different route along the sloping hill to the south to gain a high spot to cover the area.

Clay followed Captain Rice at a distance, who crept quietly up to the unsuspecting guard standing watch at the south side of the cabin. The snap of a twig underfoot caught the guard's attention. Ice shot through Clay's veins, but as the guard twisted to face the intruders, Captain Rice jumped into action. He swung the butt of his rifle against the guard's head. With quick efficiency, he caught the now unconscious man before he dropped, quietly lowered him to the ground, and hand-cuffed him.

CHAPTER FORTY-SIX

Panting hysterically, Liberty closed her eyes. She centered herself and slowed her breathing. If she was going to survive this and save her mother, she had to control herself.

Around Pete, she saw Judith nock another arrow. She said something to Rick out of the corner of her mouth, and Rick nodded with trepidation. Liberty got the sense that it had to do with being upset with Pete's interference.

Movement near the corner of the house caught Liberty's attention. She glanced that way, trying not to bring attention, and saw a man in black with a rifle. His back was planted against the wall of the house, and from behind his right shoulder, a familiar face peered. *Can it be?*

Judith pulled back the arrow.

In one swift motion, Liberty pushed the rope up and over her head with one hand and lunged for the gun in Pete's pants. Her hand clasped the pistol while Pete's hand closed over hers with a vise grip that kept her from drawing it. Liberty resorted to the next best thing. She moved her finger down and squeezed the trigger.

Boom!

The gun jumped in her hand, and the bullet shot into Pete's leg. Blood exploded out the back of his thigh. Pete collapsed, groaning in pain. Judith released the arrow, but the gunshot must have startled her because her aim was off. It missed JJ completely. Then chaos erupted.

CHAPTER FORTY-SEVEN

Gunshots rang out, and Clay focused his attention on Judith and Rick Pines. Judith's head snapped back, her feet shuffled, and she turned to Rick with a confused look on her face.

"Mom?" Rick cried.

Clay saw the blood running from the bullet hole in Judith's forehead, down the side of her nose, and along a wrinkle to the bottom of her face. Body convulsing, she attempted to speak, but nothing came out. Judith dropped to her knees and toppled over.

More bullets flew, and Rick ran for cover behind a wooden column. Three of Rick's guards were firing their guns in a frenzy. One of them yelped, and his body shook from the automatic fire riddling his chest. Another guard hid behind an old BBQ grill, and the last one ran into the forest.

Rick's gun hand stuck out from behind the wooden column and fired at a SWAT officer only ten feet away. Bullets hit the officer's protected chest, but one round pierced his neck, spurting blood. The man fell as another officer ran in. With precise aim, he filled Rick's body with automatic lead. As the bullets exited his body, they splintered the wood of the post behind him, spitting shrapnel out the back.

The officer dove for cover around the corner of the house as Clay witnessed automatic fire erupt from behind the BBQ grill ahead of them.

Clay motioned to Hank and pointed at the grill as the guard moved from behind his hiding spot. Hank pelted the barbecue with three shots from his shotgun. Several pellets checkered the guard's shoulder, and he shrieked in pain, but it didn't stop his gunfire. The guard reloaded his weapon and fired several shots in their direction.

Clay swore as a bullet pierced his leg. It went in and out the back, and he was forced to shelter himself behind the house. The officer who'd taken out Rick crept around the opposite corner of the house to sight the BBQ man. That guard turned and fired shots into the wooden wall protecting the officer, spitting splinters into his hands.

Hank and Clay fired at the guard again, and when the man poked his head out to fire back, the sniper shot one dead center through his head. It was all over in seconds, but Clay knew that Liberty and JJ were still in danger.

"Liberty!" Clay hollered, then a shot fired at him.

"Don't come any closer!" Jon Grinder commanded.

CHAPTER FORTY-EIGHT

Pete was on his back, and Liberty was on top of him, her back pressed against his chest as Pete pinned her to him with his free arm. She wrestled and fought to escape, but Pete's arms were steel. He pressed the hot muzzle to her temple, and she heard the sizzle and smelled burning flesh before feeling the sting of its touch.

"Stop your wrestling, Libby."

She obeyed.

Using Liberty as his shield, Pete scooted toward the forest with his legs. He dug each foot into the ground and pushed. Pete grunted with effort and groaned in pain. He reached a small decline, and they slid down through leaves and branches.

"Give it up!" Hank called. "You got nowhere to go!"

Pete didn't answer.

Liberty kept her eyes on her mom. JJ was a good distance away, but Liberty could see that JJ was struggling to free herself from the arrow pinning her to the hay bale. She'd finally busted loose of the tape that'd held her wrists together. She worked on the ropes with one good hand since the arrow pierced the left one. JJ loosened the ropes, but because of the long shaft sticking out, she couldn't get them completely off her.

"Come on, Mom," Liberty prayed.

Liberty and Pete passed the hill that JJ was stuck on. Once they moved into a copse of trees, JJ was out of Liberty's sight.

"Ahhhh!" JJ's scream was as much a yell of pain as it was a war cry. There was so much determination in her tone that it gave Liberty hope. She had to believe that JJ was pulling that arrow out of her arm but couldn't imagine how excruciating that would be.

Pete hit rocks and large branches but scooted fast along the ground. He was surrounded by the cover of trees. Liberty was still pinned to his chest, and Pete kept the muzzle against her head. She didn't dare make a move. Pete paused for a minute. His chest pumped up and down fast beneath her, and he panted for air. They started to move again. He scooted two more feet, slid another three down a slope, then stopped. Someone stood over them.

Liberty craned her head to see her mom glowering down at Pete. At that angle, she was tall and fierce. With both hands, JJ held a log the size of an arm, and her upper lip curled into a snarl.

Pete was moving the pistol to aim at JJ when the log hammered down so close to Liberty that she flinched. The wood smashed against Pete's forearm with a crack. The gun went off as she struck, then the pistol flew from his hand. His grip on her loosened, and Liberty rolled off Pete just as JJ swung the log against Pete's head. The back of Pete's skull slammed against the ground.

"Not my daughter, *asshole*," JJ said with a finite tone.

JJ gritted her teeth as she once again brought the log down onto his face with a massive force. She lifted it for another blow, smashed again, rose again, and smashed again. Blood spattered the log and the ground around it.

Crouching next to Pete, Liberty stared in awe at his limp body and unrecognizable face. His head was a mangled red pulp.

"Mom!" Liberty cried and leaped to her feet.

JJ released the log from her shaking hands and collapsed into Liberty.

"Liberty!" Clay's voice called from somewhere close by.

Are you okay? Liberty's conscious whispered.

"Over here!" Liberty strangled through tears. "Hurry!"

Liberty sat on the ground with her mother's head in her lap. JJ, eyes closed, was unconscious. Her mouth hung open and saliva dripped from her bottom lip. Liberty sobbed as Clay ran to them. He bent over

JJ. A bloody hole blossomed on her chest. Below the arrow wound in her shoulder, Pete's bullet had pierced its target—a few inches to the right of the center of her chest.

"Ambulance is on the way." Clay looked at JJ with pain-stricken eyes as he quickly tore off his shirt and pressed it against the wound.

All Liberty could do was weep while holding her mother. The fear of losing her clogged any words in her throat from escaping. Clay pressed all his weight against the wound as blood seeped through his white shirt.

JJ's face started to lose color, and Liberty raised her wet eyes to him. "I c-can't lose her."

"You're not going to." Clay locked eyes with Liberty. He twisted his head behind him and yelled, "Are they here yet?"

A tall man with a handlebar mustache trotted up to them with his hands full of gauze. Clay appeared to know him. He was possibly Clay's partner. "They just pulled up. They're comin'. Here." He knelt, replaced Clay's bloody shirt with the gauze pads, and pressed his weight on her wounds.

"Mom," Liberty pleaded, "please come back. Come back. *Fight.* You did for so long. Just do it a few minutes longer."

Two officers ran down the hill, followed by two paramedics carrying equipment. Clay reached over and clasped Liberty's arm.

"She's going to be fine," he assured her.

Liberty's head spun. They stepped back to allow the paramedics in to work on JJ, and she turned to look at Clay. "He said you were *dead.*"

"Still here." He shrugged with a grin. He rubbed the wound on his forehead. "Came really close though."

Liberty's eyes wandered down his body. Blood stained the side of his face and neck, his arm was a mangled, bleeding mess, and his leg had been shot up too. "Is there anywhere on you that he missed?" Liberty half chuckled.

"Just... my finger feels all right." Clay smiled while showing his index finger.

"Thank you." Liberty's bottom lip quivered, and she collapsed into his arms, burying her face in his chest.

Clay wrapped his good arm around her and held her tight.

"I'm glad you're still here," she said. "Very glad."

"I'm glad you are too."

CHAPTER FORTY-NINE

"*T*ime"
  With each passing day, I have finally learned that I can't fix you.

  Only you have the power to change your life...

  Time has taught me forgiveness and that we all deserve a second chance.

  Here's to our second chance.

-Poem from Liberty Justice's Diary

The paramedics were thorough and fast, and they delivered JJ to the hospital in record time. While JJ was in surgery, doctors checked out Liberty and attended to her wounds. Besides dehydration, she made out with only minor cuts, bruises, and the burn on her temple. When she was finished, she headed straight for her mother's room and waited for JJ to return from surgery.

Three hours later, two nurses wheeled her mother in. JJ was still unconscious. Danielle, a young brunette nurse, attended to her.

Danielle glanced at Liberty. "You've been through hell."

"You could say that."

Liberty turned her eyes to her mom, who lay unmoving in the bed. She had an IV attached to her wrist, and her shoulder and arm were bandaged. Her stringy hair was dirty, and it splayed out across the pillow. Dark shadows were around her eyes, and her cheeks looked sunken in. Her left cheek was swollen and bruised from where Pete had hit her.

"What kind of soda would you like?" Danielle asked.

"What?"

"Soda, juice, or water. Whatever you want. I'll go get it for you. Some snacks too. You've been here all day, and you probably need something."

"I'm fine."

"I'm going to bring something back for you anyway. Might as well tell me what you like."

"Coke?"

"You got it." Danielle winked and left the room.

Liberty sat in silence, the only sound the constant beep of machines.

Are you okay?

I don't know. We'll see.

She felt safe but couldn't trust it. She wanted to believe it was all over and that they were out of danger, but it was hard for her body to readjust. The killer, Jon Grinder, was dead. And the fact that Pete was gone for good was a bonus. What scratched Liberty's brain and nerves was the thought that he'd been her biological father. She had to ask her mom to verify, but JJ was out, and she didn't know when she would wake up. And once JJ did, she might not be all there.

If he is your dad, do you wish he was still alive?

No!

It's okay. You can tell me the truth.

It is the truth, she told her conscience defiantly.

Do you wish you had more time with him?

What? So he could beat me? Give me a break.

Are you afraid?

Liberty shifted in her chair. *Afraid of what?*

That he's a part of you? You could carry his traits.

I'd like to think I'm more like my mom.

Liberty didn't know how to process her thoughts about Pete. It made her sick to think of some of her traits, personality, or talents coming from *that* man. But it was what it was, and she was inevitably from him. It all created a giant confusion ball of spaghetti in her head that she couldn't unwind.

"Here you go, sweetie." Danielle entered with a cup of ice, a straw, a can of coke, and an armful of treats consisting of crackers and peanuts. "This will put something in your belly. I made sure there's some protein in your snacks." She set it all down on the table next to JJ's bed.

"Thank you."

"You're welcome. You need anything, you just ring for me, okay? Just call me Dani." Dani smiled and left the room.

A few minutes later, JJ woke up. She spoke a few jumbled, nonsensical words before she went back out. But before slipping into slumber again, JJ did form a smile and said, "Love you." That was enough for Liberty for the moment. There'd been a sparkle in JJ's eyes that Liberty hadn't seen in years. It brought her back to thunderstorms and watermelon.

An hour later, Liberty awoke to her mother's voice. Liberty had dozed off in the chair next to her mom's bed.

"Liberty?" JJ spoke softly.

Liberty cracked her eyes open then shot up straight when she saw her mom leaning over the bed. "Mom? Are you okay?"

JJ smiled. "I'm fine. Been better, but... how are you?"

"Me? Yeah, I'm fine."

"He didn't hurt you, did he?"

"Not really. You saved my life."

"You saved mine. I guess we're square," JJ said.

"So... is it true? Is Pete really my father?"

JJ sighed and shrugged. "Yes, he is."

Liberty nodded and looked down.

"I'm sorry," JJ said.

"At first, I was angry. Furious would be the better word. But once I had time to think about it, I see why you never told me."

"I'm sorry you never knew. You never got a chance to know him as your dad."

"I wanted a dad, just not *him*."

"He wasn't capable of being a father."

"It's just... when you have a monster like him in your life—someone who damaged our family and who took so much away from us—to find out he's your father and that you're part him..." Liberty shook her head. "I don't know what to think."

"Pete had some good traits. He wasn't all bad. Fortunately, you got the good parts. And yes, you are a little of me and a little of him, but you are mostly *you*. You still get to make your choices in life. You have so much talent, intelligence, and beauty. What you choose to do with that is entirely up to you."

Tears ran, and Liberty's heart filled with love and comfort. "Sometimes you really know the right things to say."

"I'm your mom. I'm supposed to."

Liberty leaned into her open arms for a hug, and they held each other for a long time.

"Hello?" Serene said as she and Joe stepped into the room. "Hi, Jemma. Hi, Liberty."

They all greeted and hugged each other. Serene and Joe visited with JJ for a good ten minutes before JJ's eyes dragged closed.

"We better leave you. Let you get your rest." Serene turned to walk away, hesitated, then turned and kissed JJ on her forehead. "Love ya, sis."

The three exited the room. Aunt Serene, Uncle Joe, and Liberty walked to the waiting room and sat down. Normally, they would have reprimanded Liberty for running away and stealing their car. Liberty had half expected that. But instead, they wrapped their arms around her. Hugging her aunt and uncle, feeling their warmth and acceptance, overwhelmed Liberty. That was family. Something she hadn't experienced in a long time.

Clay appeared from around the corner in a wheelchair, rolling into the small waiting room where Liberty sat with Serene and Joe. His arm was wrapped and cradled in a sling, and his leg was set in a cast up past his thigh.

"You look like shit." Liberty chuckled, and Clay rolled his eyes.

"I feel like shit. How's your mom doing?"

"She pulled through surgery. Now she's resting."

Her uncle stepped up. "Hi. I'm Joe, and this is my wife, Serene." He reached a hand to Clay, who shook it.

"Detective Clay Baxter."

"He's the one who saved us," Liberty said.

"Liberty, can I talk to you alone for a moment?" He turned to Serene and Joe. "Would that be all right?"

"Sure. Of course," Joe said and turned to his wife. "Let's go down to the gift shop and pick something out. Give them some time."

She nodded, and they left. Clay rolled closer to Liberty.

"So, you going to be mummified for a while?" Liberty chuckled.

"Looks that way. It could have been a lot worse. Course, the doctors always tell you how close to death you came."

"I think they say that so it makes it look like they saved your life." Liberty smirked.

"Yeah, I think so. They said the same about the bullet that nearly hit your mom's heart. But in that case, her surviving really is a miracle."

"Yes," Liberty agreed. "And I owe you big-time for my mom's life. And mine."

"You *do* owe me one." His lips spread in a large grin. "I took a couple of bullets for you. Of course, it could have all been avoided if you had told me you were at the Sleep Inn Motel." He gave her a friendly wink, and she shrugged.

"I don't know how you found us."

"It wasn't easy, but it's like I said before. Someone upstairs is looking out for you."

Liberty nodded. "So, what happens now?"

"Looks like your mom's going to be fine. She'll be in here for a while, and it'll be miserable, but she's got the best medical care. She'll get through it. I talked to the DA about an hour ago. There's no evidence that you killed Billy Ray Pines. The knife doesn't have either your or your mom's prints. So that's good. But your mom ran from authorities, and he wants to press a number of charges against her."

"Hey! Hold on. You said—"

"I know what I said. I can't make any guarantees, though, but this is a good thing. He's willing to drop all charges if she agrees to go into rehab."

Liberty was silent as the wheels turned in her head.

"It's the best way to get her to go. What do you think? Will she do it?" Clay asked.

"She better. I'll make her, or I'm gone."

"Good. I'm glad to hear that. I think that will work."

They sat in awkward silence for a moment, then Clay said, "So, do you have a place to go?"

"Aunt Serene and Uncle Joe will take me in. They live in Langston."

"That's a bit of a ways."

"Yeah. I'll have to start a new school. Again." She shook her head. "New friends. Oh, joy." She frowned.

"I know how tough changing schools can be. I could talk to them. See if they'd let you stay at my place. At least until the end of the school year. I-I could, uh, take you down there on the weekends or something. You know, if that's okay with you. If you want to, I mean."

Her eyes lit up. "Really? You'd do that? You'd want to?" She scrunched her face.

"Well, yeah, of course. You can show me more of that poetry you write." Clay smiled.

"Thank you again for what you did. You were a real friend out there when I needed one. I felt so alone."

"You're a good friend to have," Clay admitted. "So, what do you say? You wanna try it? Plus, you'll be closer to your mom. I'll take you to visit her when she's able to have visitors."

"Hell yeah, I'm in." She beamed.

THE DA WAS GOOD TO his word and presented JJ and her court-appointed attorney the deal. He also added the fact that CPS would investigate her living conditions, and she could lose custody of Liberty if she didn't get help. JJ paused for a moment, and Liberty clenched every muscle in her body. Her mom could go either way. If JJ said no, everything would blow apart. Liberty was empty of trying and fighting.

At last, her mom finally said, "Yes, I'll do it."

She couldn't tell if it was out of surrender or triumph, but Liberty would take the yes any way she could.

Liberty was filled with so many emotions as they approached the rehab center. Every nerve tingled from the end of her fingers to the tips of her toes. She was sad and hopeful at the same time. That day was equal parts good and bad. She was losing her mom for a short time to gain her for a longer time. That was what she kept telling herself.

Serene and Joe parked the Escape next to the curb by the front doors of the center, and everyone slowly exited. JJ dragged her suitcase behind and looked up at the sign, which read Hopeful Solutions. The name was proper since hope was all Liberty had to hang on to. Blood drained from JJ's face, and she turned to her daughter.

"You've got this, Mom." Liberty choked back tears. She didn't know if she was ready to say goodbye or to be without her for three months—or however long it took. She couldn't imagine how hard it was for her mom.

JJ let out a breath, and a smile crept on her lips. "You're something else, kiddo. You know that?"